Suki stared into his gray eyes defiantly

"I don't think it's my opinion of myself that bothers you," she retorted. "It's my opinion of you." Joel Harlow's face stiffened, but Suki continued, "I think you're a man who's always had everything he wanted and has come to believe he's entitled to reach out a hand for anything he fancies."

He laughed, low and angry. "Charming," he said. "But do go on."

Suki smiled sweetly. "Mr. Harlow, I get the feeling we're playing some sort of truth game—but a dangerous one."

"The truth's always dangerous. Normally I wouldn't meddle with it," he said. "I'd realize you didn't like me and walk away without a backward glance."

"Then why don't you do just that?" she demanded rudely.

His answer was brief and direct. "Because I want you too badly."

CHARLOTTE LAMB

the girl from nowhere

Harlequin Books

TORONTO • LONDON • LOS ANGELES • AMSTERDAM
SYDNEY • HAMBURG • PARIS • STOCKHOLM • ATHENS • TOKYO

Harlequin Presents edition published January 1982
ISBN 0-373-10478-2

Original hardcover edition published in 1981
by Mills & Boon Limited

CHAPTER ONE

LAST night she had dreamt about it, her mind preparing her for this moment, but nothing could have prepared her for how it actually felt. She stood in the shadowy corridor, listening to the distant sea-like roar, waiting for the introduction. She was feeling sick, her stomach tense, all her muscles cramped. It was a feeling she knew well. She always had stage fright before she went on, but tonight it was worse than anything she had ever known before.

'Okay?' Buddy leaned against the wall beside her, his hands in his pockets, watching her, all his attention fixed on her.

Suki didn't answer, she just nodded, her eyes riveted on the floor. Buddy was worried, he was always worried before she went on, he knew exactly how she would be feeling; her palms damp with perspiration, her mouth dry, that sensation of sick dread deep in the pit of her stomach.

'Feel bad?' he pressed, giving her a shrewd look.

Suki's face was white under her heavy stage make-up. She wondered if she would ever stop having these moments of panic before a performance. Her green eyes had dilated, the black pupils enormous and her upper lip was dewed with beads of sweat.

'Relax,' said Buddy, patting her cheek. 'Everything's going to be just fine.'

The applause faded slightly, they heard the crackle of the microphone on the tannoy above their heads, and then the build-up began.

'You're on,' Buddy said, but she didn't move, her body rigid, locked in terror. It seemed an eternity, but it could only have been a few seconds before she straightened and lifted her head, the automatic pilot inside her numbed brain taking over.

Taking a stumbling step, she began to walk. The corridor seemed to stretch endlessly. That was how it had felt in the dream, she had heard the sounds in the distance, the waves of applause breaking on the shore of her mind, the lit emptiness of the huge stage swimming in front of her at the end of the echoing tunnel. She had known she wasn't going to make it, she wasn't going to be able to walk out there, and she had frozen in immobility, her whole body clenched in fear. Then she had woken up, sweating, a cry of panic breaking from her.

Although she was aware of Buddy following at her heels, his watchful gaze always on her, she ignored him, her mind set on what she had to do, and she had the inward-turning look of someone daring to look neither to left nor to right, doggedly walking on because they have no choice. Tonight she kept on walking, and the light came closer and the noise grew and grew until she walked out into that deep-throated roar of welcome, her curved body swaying with sensuous grace under the clinging, glittering dress.

'Hallo, everybody!'

She stood at the microphone, her arms stretched out in an embrace which invited them all, not seeing any faces in the great auditorium, but feeling them there, reaching out towards her in their turn, the applause mounting until it totally enveloped her.

'You have a love affair with your fans,' Buddy had once said to her shrewdly. 'Every time you go out on the stage you're making love to them.' Suki had laughed at the time, but she had known deep inside herself that he had hit the nail on the head. The waves of feeling came out to her and washed back again from her to the unseen faces, the anonymous demanding lovers she would never meet.

The orchestra broke into one of her most famous hits and the audience reacted delightedly as Suki began to sing. For the first few bars her voice had the faintest quiver, then as she surfaced from her state of panic her adrenalin flowed like quicksilver in her veins and she began to give out at full power. She felt the quickening in them out there and smiled, her tensely lifted head glittering like golden fire under the spotlight.

Behind her sat the orchestra, buried in shadow, so that they should not distract the audience from her. Her backing group sang at a row of microphones to one side of the stage. All day this vast place had been filled with activity; carpenters, electricians, sound engineers working away from early in the morning until shortly before the audience flooded into the seats.

They had done their job; now it was her turn, and the feeling of love between her and the unseen faces lifted her up as the performance began to build to the interval climax. From where Suki stood the audience was a black wall, the crash of their appreciation rising to the roof whenever she finished a song or began another. She had to sing into that wall, project herself towards them almost physically, her smooth skin glowing softly in the lights, the skin-tight dress emphasising her air of smouldering provocation, the millions of tiny silver scales from low shoulderline to hem giving off dancing reflections.

Buddy was waiting as she came off, her eyes brilliant, her body strung up with excitement. He put an arm around her and walked her to the dressing-room to change for the second half. She was covered in perspiration and showered before she got into the black dress. Milly looked at her in the mirror, grimacing.

'You look terrible!'

'You're such a comfort!' Suki felt the long zipper slide smoothly upwards. Milly's fingers were incredibly deft considering she had atrocious arthritis. She still had lingering bronchitis, too, after the bitter winter; Suki could hear the heavy drag of her breathing as she adjusted the hang of the bodice. She smiled at Milly in the mirror.

'How do you think it's going?'

'They're eating you,' said Milly with flat satisfaction. 'Now don't start too high when you go out there again or you know you'll never get back up again before the last song.'

'Nag, nag, nag,' smiled Suki, kissing her cheek before she went out as the tannoy crackled out her name. Milly had been with her for the last two years, they had an easy relationship, and were used to each other. Milly never overwhelmed her with compliments. She had been dressing stars all her working life, if you believed her. She had seen them come and she had seen them go, and she refused to be impressed by anybody. Small, grey, wiry and tart of tongue, she did her job and then she went home to her husband, her little bungalow and her two Siamese cats, forgetting the glamour and the tinsel excitement of show business. Milly was, she often said, a realist. Suki had found her grim common sense very comforting during the past two years. Milly had been an anchor for her when the accelerating whirl of success threatened to sweep her away with it.

Buddy had discovered Milly for her after she had a series of rather alarming incidents when fans or admirers tried to break into her home or sneak into her dressing-room.

'You need a bodyguard,' he had told her.

'I've got you.'

'I meant someone who'll be around all day when you're working, chaperone you, keep people away.'

'When I'm working you're always there,' Suki had pointed out, but Buddy had sighed and shaken his head.

'Your own dresser, that's what you need.' So he had gone off and found Milly who, from then on, had stuck to her like glue during the day. In the evenings she had Buddy and Rosie, of course. She was never alone.

Sometimes she had a brief, faint rebellion over that, needing to be alone, feeling a craving for it, and then she usually disguised herself with dark glasses and a wig and went for a drive alone. She had a white Ferrari which ate the miles once they hit the motorway, the speed giving her the same sort of adrenalin she got when she was out there on stage, singing.

Buddy looked at her dress with a mixture of approval and dismay. 'You ought to wear a bra under that.'

'I can't.' The designer had made that blatantly obvious when she first tried the dress on, shaking his head with an aggressive expression. 'From out front it will hardly show that I'm not, anyway,' she added.

Buddy wasn't convinced, but he took another look, saying: 'It's certainly sensational.'

'It ought to be—it cost a fortune.'

'I know, I signed the cheque,' Buddy grimaced.

Through the black lace of the bodice the smooth gleam of her breasts showed subtly, the black satin underslip giving just sufficient support to emphasise the firm uplift of the pale flesh. The bodice was merely two black shells clipped together across the deep cleft of white skin between her breasts. The skirt was moulded to her until it reached the deep, flaring ruffles of lace which began halfway down her calf.

'Don't walk too fast or that will split,' said Buddy, and Suki grinned at him.

'They'd love that!'

'Maybe, but remember how much it cost,' he retorted.

'Cheap-skate!' she told him as she left him to go back out there to where her fans were yelling for her. She had never given a concert like this one—it was vast. She knew it was in the nature of a recognition. She had arrived, she wouldn't be here if she had not reached the very top, and that was enough to send that wave of adrenalin through anybody's veins, but to Suki it was not the money, the fame, the publicity that mattered. It was those people out there. If you were to put over a song with passion, conviction and power, you had to believe in the music. The singer was the song, in this business. Suki did not want to forget that it was the two-way love which had taken her to the top, she did not want to harden inside, as she had seen happen to so many artistes, so that what people got was a tough, glossy shell which went right the way through to the very middle of the singer.

What meant most to her was her ability to move an audience, to know that they listened with rapt attention, her voice tapping their emotions, so that she could make them smile or bring tears to their eyes, make them dance or make them go crazy with the sheer beat of the sound. She would lose that magic power if she lost her own ability to feel deeply, if she ever stopped giving herself openly, with both hands, everything alive in her flowing with the song.

As the performance went on the feeling was electric, her energy burning out under the lights, her slender sensual body moving like a gyrating puppet with the people keeping up their draining, exhausting demand. One night, she thought, I'll spin myself right off the stage and fly to the moon and never come down again.

Buddy was hovering in attendance as she came off, drenched in sweat, white, shuddering, so high she felt manic as he grabbed her and flung a dressing-gown round her.

He kissed her on both cheeks, his thin face high-coloured. 'You were wonderful, baby, you were wonderful!'

She hugged him, half blind with the perspiration

trickling into her eyes from her forehead, a faint streak
of mascara running from the corner of one eye so that
she looked like a sad French clown. Flinging off the
dressing-gown, she ran back to take another tumul-
tous wave of applause, kissing her hands to them,
turning to applaud the orchestra and then the backing
group. It was all a ritual they went through every time,
the movements of it practised and rehearsed, yet each
time when it came to that moment she felt it happened
spontaneously, on impulse, a fresh explosion of happiness and shared achievement between them all.

The last time she came off Buddy said: 'Enough is
enough,' and firmly took her back to her dressing-
room. She sat down in front of the mirror and looked
at herself, laughing.

'Don't I look a sight!' She sang off-key: 'If they
could see me now . . .'

Buddy pushed a glass into her hand. 'Drink this and
shut up. You've done enough singing.'

Suki sipped the brandy, grimacing. Milly unzipped
her, she stood up and let the dress peel off and slide
to the floor where Milly gathered it up tenderly and
carried it away over her arm. Standing there in her
tiny black panties, a brief black towelling robe tied
round her, Suki finished her drink and went off to
have a shower. Buddy talked at her every step of the
way until she turned on him and asked sarcastically:
'You taking a shower with me, are you?'

'He would, given half a chance,' said a voice at the
door and Suki grinned.

'Hi, Rosie.'

Rosie was thin and elegant and wry, her blue eyes

faintly cynical, her silvery-rinsed hair beautifully styled. She and Buddy had been married for fifteen years and knew each other intimately, without illusion.

'Not so much a love affair, more a tax dodge,' Rosie used to joke, and some people seemed to think she wasn't being funny. Rosie had that sardonic look, especially when she talked about Buddy, but as Suki got to know her from living with her for months she had come to realise that, with or without illusions about him, Rosie loved Buddy, she needed him.

'We belong together,' she had once admitted to Suki. 'Like Jekyll and Hyde.'

'Which half am I?' Buddy had asked, and Rosie had said sweetly: 'That is what's known as leading with your chin.'

Now she said: 'I've never heard you sing better. The electricity was so strong I thought you were going to fuse every plug in the works.'

'Thank you,' said Suki, going into the cubicle and pulling the door shut. She showered slowly, taking her time, feeling the water wash away all the stale scent and perspiration like a discarded snakeskin. It was one of her favourite moments and she lingered over it, eyes closed, head beating with the music which was now silent.

As she stepped out, dripping, Milly enveloped her in an enormous fluffy white towel. Buddy was sitting on a chair with his feet propped on the wall. Rosie was drinking a glass of whisky. leaning on the wall.

'You look ultra-smart,' Suki commented, eyeing her black dress.

'Who'll notice?' Rosie murmured.

'I will,' Buddy promised, and she gave him a smile, blowing him a kiss at the same time. Buddy lifted one foot and waved it at her.

'Coming to the party, Milly?' Rosie asked.

'Not me,' said Milly, her mouth turning down at the edges. 'Got better things to do with my time.' She helped Suki into the trouser suit she had chosen for the party, clicking her tongue. 'If you had any sense you'd go back to bed too.'

'You know it takes her hours to get back down to earth after a show,' said Buddy.

'I'm as high as a loose balloon,' Suki agreed, peering at herself in the mirror. Her eyes glittered and her face had an elated tension in it. She whirled and hugged Milly. 'Come on, come to my party, you old gloombox.'

'Get off!' protested Milly, wriggling away and glaring. 'Sit down and let me do your face. I want to get home to my cats.'

'Not to her husband, you notice,' Buddy observed to his feet, doing a little tap dance with them on the wall.

'My husband's fast asleep by now,' Milly told him. 'He always is by ten o'clock.'

'Married to you, so would I be,' grinned Buddy.

'And stop making the wall dirty,' Milly scolded.

Someone pounded on the door. Milly went over and opened it a crack. 'No, she's not ready yet,' she said, slamming it again at once.

'Who was that?' Suki enquired, staring at herself in the mirror.

'Nobody.'

'Oh, him,' shrugged Rosie, finishing her whisky and

putting down the glass.

Under Milly's quick, clever fingers Suki watched her pale tired face disappear and a new, glowing vital face appear.

'Magic!' she said.

Milly sniffed, not to be won over with soft words. She took her time putting the vivid red-gold hair into place again and Suki sat patiently until she was told she could move.

'Well, I'm off then,' said Milly, moving to the door, and Suki said: 'Not yet, have a glass of champagne, Milly, just one with me, go on.'

Buddy had swung to his feet and was uncorking the bottle. It popped and everyone laughed, and Rosie picked up the cork and handed it to Milly with a little smile at Suki.

'What am I supposed to do with that?' Milly asked, pushing it into her pocket.

'Wear it,' said Buddy, handing her a glass filled with winking bubbles.

When they all had glasses, Buddy said: 'Suki,' and they lifted their glasses to her. The pounding had begun again. Rosie went to the door this time, said sweetly: 'Run away, there's good boys,' and shut it again.

'Did you see Al put his foot through the bass drum?' Buddy asked Suki, who shrieked: 'No, he didn't?'

'Monk's a bit flat on the lower register,' said Rosie, and Buddy grimaced: 'Yes, I noticed that, I'll have words with him.'

Milly said again: 'I'm off,' and Suki kissed her. 'Thanks, Milly, you're wonderful.' Milly stumped off to the door.

'Shall I let them in?' she asked as she opened it, and Suki nodded.

'Yes, let them all come in now,' said Rosie, tipping her glass and swallowing the last of her champagne. 'The bar's open.'

'I really thought I'd split that dress when I was singing "Fire Song",' Suki told Buddy.

'I thought you'd fall on your face,' he said. 'How do you manage to dance in that thing? I'm surprised you can move at all.'

The door was filled with people, talking, exclaiming, rushing at her, and the performance began all over again in a different key as she smiled, accepted kisses, hugged people, listened while they sang her praises, made jokes and pretended to laugh at old ones she had heard a hundred times before.

They went on to a nightclub an hour later. Buddy had cleverly weeded out the people they wanted from the others. Suki often wondered how he did it. It was all so deft, so subtle. Smiling, he led the rejected ones to the door, an arm around their shoulders, talking them out with extreme friendliness, until at last the only ones left were either real friends or people Buddy felt should be encouraged.

Buddy had been her business manager for five years. He had picked her up in a London bar, packed to the doors with teenagers, the air smoky, the throb of the rock music deafening. Buddy had wandered in for a casual drink on impulse, drawn by the sound of the music, and had stayed, watching her intently. She had been sitting on a bar stool when he first came in, a tiny slender figure in tight black leather jeans and a black shirt open to the cleft of her breasts, and she had seen him and been amused because he was so obviously out of place among their usual crowd. He was the wrong age group, a very tall, very thin, man of around forty whose jerky, disconnected movements made him look like a badly made puppet, his flyaway blond hair turning grey, his face long and pale, like a face seen in a spoon.

Suki had jumped down to do her first song, and her voice hit the air, making Buddy jump.

It had all seemed so exciting to her, then, singing with a group of energetic boys who were just a step up from amateurs. They had earned very little, but the money hadn't mattered. It had been the music which mattered even then. They were hooked on it, addicted, not even wanting to be paid. What had happened to those boys? she wondered as she leaned back in the limousine, half listening to Buddy talking, half dreaming of the past. She had never set eyes on any of them again. She hadn't a clue whether they had gone on working in music or left to get real jobs earning real money.

Buddy had stayed for the whole evening, then as she left he had come up to her. 'I've got a proposition for you,' he had said, and she had looked at him with wry distaste and disbelief.

'Get lost!'

'I'm serious, kid,' he had insisted, a hand on her arm.

Suki had shaken it off and walked away, but Buddy was not the type you shook off when he wanted something. He had followed patiently and said: 'You've got talent, more talent than I've seen all year, and if you put yourself in my hands . . .'

'Look, granddad,' Suki had muttered, through her teeth, 'I don't want to know. Why don't you go and find someone your own age?'

Buddy had laughed under his breath, pulling out a card from his inside pocket. 'Here's my address. Look me up, check on me, then come and see me. You're wasted on this collection of guitar cowboys.' He had pushed the card into her hand and reluctantly she had accepted it. 'And by the way,' Buddy had added, 'my wife runs the business with me and if I so much as looked at you she'd cut my throat.'

He hadn't been joking, as Suki realised when she did take the risk of visiting his office a week later, and met Rosie.

'Buddy tells me you were suspicious,' Rosie had said frankly. 'I'm sure you had good reason. I can't stop him using his eyes, but if he starts trying to do any touching, I'll sew him up in a mailbag and chuck him in the Thames.'

'Strictly business,' Buddy had promised, holding up protesting hands.

Suki hadn't quite believed him then. It had taken time for her to trust him.

She surfaced as they reached the entrance of the nightclub. Buddy was saying dreamily: 'A tour of the States.'

'She isn't going this year,' said Rosie.

'Too many other bookings,' Buddy agreed. 'Next spring, though.' He climbed out of the car and handed Suki out on to the pavement.

'My husband, the gentleman,' Rosie drawled as he turned away, and he helped her out, patting her rear lovingly.

'Sorry, buttercup.'

'He's drunk,' Rosie told Suki.

'Not yet,' said Buddy. 'But I'm going to be.'

They went into the nightclub in a noisy, laughing crowd, and people craned and whispered and stared while the head waiter bowed them to a table on which the champagne already waited in a silver ice bucket. The cork popped and the straw-coloured wine bubbled into glasses. The group playing stared at them and people leaned over to talk to Suki, praising her again, making jokes about the show.

'Let's dance,' Buddy told her, dragging her to her feet.

'Can I borrow your husband?' she asked Rosie, who gave one of her elegant little shrugs.

'Be my guest.'

'We'll all dance,' said Buddy, laughing.

'Not me,' Rosie said firmly. 'I'm not with you.'

'Come on!' said Suki, eager now to move to the music. Buddy laughed at her as she danced round him, the brilliant blue of the trouser suit flashing. It was more a stage costume than anything she normally wore, but tonight was special. She had known she would be in public tonight and she had dressed to be noticed. The silk material was sewn with pearly glittering sequins which flashed like mirrors as she moved.

'Showy, isn't it?' Buddy asked, and she lifted her bright head with a defiant smile.

'I like it.' It was how she felt tonight, she felt elated, euphoric, like someone walking on the sky.

'When you come down you're going to come with a thump,' Buddy observed.

'Don't rain on my parade,' she told him, and he kissed her cheek, laughing.

As he moved away she danced off lightly, body moving in perfect time with the music, and across the crowded nightclub met a pair of steely grey eyes. For some reason they were like a douche of cold water to her in that exhilarated state of mind. She only looked at the man briefly before looking away, but his image remained imprinted on her inner vision: a hard, unsmiling face, thick black hair brushed down almost to his white shirt collar, a strong jawline and a mouth which was beautifully cut but firmly under control.

Rosie was waving from their table. 'Come and get it,' she said as Suki joined her. The supper they had ordered had arrived and Suki sank into her chair with a reluctant sigh. She wasn't hungry. Her mind was too blown. The thought of food made her feel sick and she looked at it with distaste.

'Eat,' said Rosie, reading her mind.

'I can't.'

'Do I have to feed you, for mercy's sake?'

'She would,' Buddy warned.

'Come on, unwind,' Rosie coaxed. 'Do you want to pop right out of your head?'

Someone picked up her fork and gave it to her, and Suki gave Rosie a sulky look. 'Why am I surrounded by nanny-types?'

'Because we're what you need, baby,' Rosie told her.

That was why they had persuaded Suki to move in and live with them. She had been seventeen when they found her and Rosie had been horrified at the idea of her staying on alone in the grotty little room she had had in a run-down part of London. It had been all she could afford and by the time Buddy and Rosie found her she had already had some pretty hairy experiences with men. Her looks made her a prime target, her lack of any family had put her at serious risk, and it had been pure luck that had taken her safely through the year she spent alone in London before she met Buddy.

She began to pick at the supper. It was melon and Parma ham, cool and refreshing. She found herself enjoying it after a while. Buddy refilled her glass and the talk around the table was lively.

Rosie glanced up and her mouth parted on an audible gasp. Suki, surprised by the sound, looked up too.

'Good evening.' The deep voice had a husky, smoky sound, but the steel grey eyes were familiar, she had seen them before a while ago when she was dancing. They had made her wild spirits flicker for a second, the impassive speculation in that stare leaving her with a startled feeling that the owner of those eyes did not approve of her.

Buddy stumbled to his feet, very flushed, an expression on his face which Suki found baffling. She had never seen Buddy look like that before; he looked, she thought, as though someone had just punched him in the stomach. She glanced away from that stupefied expression, running her eye round the table, and realised that everyone was behaving the same way, their eyes riveted on the new arrival.

Only Rosie, typically, was keeping her cool. She was smiling. 'Hallo, can we offer you a glass of champagne, Mr Harlow?'

'I came over to offer my congratulations to Miss Black,' he drawled without removing his gaze from Suki. Those grey eyes had been on her from the moment he appeared, making her nervous. When people stared at her like that, normally, she had a pretty good idea what they were thinking. Most people aren't difficult to read, their faces reflect their thoughts; they smile or frown so that you can tell if you're getting good vibes or bad, she thought. Not this man, though— his face was as readable as a brick wall.

Beaming like a wide-mouthed frog, Buddy pulled back a chair. 'Won't you join us, Mr Harlow? Have a glass of champagne to toast our star.'

Ignoring him, the man walked round towards Suki who, lowering her thick artificial black lashes, watched him through them. They all seemed to know him, but she had never seen him before, she was certain of that. If she had, she would have remembered. Who is he? she wondered.

Reaching her, he calmly took one of her hands from the table while she stiffened, blank-faced, wondering what he intended to do. Without haste or any apparent sense of being watched by everyone around them, he lifted her hand to his mouth, brushing his lips against her warm skin, his eyes looking down into her own. Dazedly Suki stared back at him, a quiver of startled reaction running down her back.

'I caught your concert tonight,' he said softly. 'You

were incredible. I thought the whole audience was going to catch fire from you.'

She swallowed, forgetting everyone else at the table, trapped for a second in a strange isolation with him, conscious of a dominant will behind that hard-boned face and feeling it concentrated on her in a way which troubled her.

'Thank you, I'm glad you enjoyed it.' The words were automatic, coming out jerkily in a nervous little voice.

Buddy had poured a glass of champagne and was holding it out to him. 'Sit down and join us, Mr Harlow,' he almost pleaded.

'I'm sorry, I'm with friends,' the other man said, straightening and releasing Suki's fingers. He looked down at her again briefly and she glanced away, a tremor of recoil running through her.

'Goodnight,' he said in that deep, smoky voice, as though he barely recognised the presence of anyone else around the table.

'Goodnight,' Suki said, wide-eyed, asking herself why it was that she felt the very way he said that to be somehow a threat. It was a polite little gesture, nothing more. Already tonight she had had brief words with dozens of strangers or casual acquaintances, accepting their praise, smiling at them as they told her how much they had enjoyed the concert. Why on earth did this man's cool words make her feel alarmed?'

He walked away, followed by the stares of everyone at the table. Suki shivered. That tall lean body was powerfully muscled, the broad shoulders and long-legged stride making it plain that he was to be reckoned with, a dangerous adversary. He was wearing evening clothes, as were most of the men in the club, but he made the beautifully cut dark suit look very different. Suki couldn't help noticing that as he walked back to his own table people parted for him instinctively and looked at him with a mixture of curiosity and ready smiles. Clearly, he was immediately recognisable and viewed with fascination.

'Wow!' Buddy whistled through his teeth, turning back towards her. 'You caught yourself a big fish there, darling.'

Suki looked at him, waiting for some explanation.

'There goes a billion dollars,' said Rosie in a dreamy voice, lifting her glass towards the departing back. 'What a beautiful sight walking about on two legs!'

'Who is he?' Suki asked.

The reaction around the table was as dramatic as if she had dropped a smoking bomb on the tablecloth. She heard the gasps, felt the eyes flash to her face, everyone in earshot apparently in a state of shock and incredulity.

'What did I say?' she asked, between laughter and alarm.

'What did she say, she asks?' Rosie muttered, beginning to laugh.

'You're joking!' Buddy's jaw had dropped visibly.

'She isn't,' said Rosie, staring at her. 'Not a sign of a twinkle. My life, Suki, sometimes I wonder if you live in the same world as the rest of us.'

Suki laughed. 'He's famous, I gather.'

'Famous?' Buddy put his head in both hands, moved it from side to side, wailing under his breath.

'Is he famous, she says?'

Rosie leaned towards her, smiling. 'Darling, that man is Joel Harlow.' She paused expectantly, waiting.

'Who's Joel Harlow?' Suki asked, still unenlightened.

'I don't believe it,' said Buddy. 'I just don't believe anyone like her exists.'

Rosie looked at her with a crooked grin. 'Come down off your ivory tower and join the rest of us. Joel Harlow is one of the richest men on the world.'

'He practically owns Fort Knox,' Buddy put in. 'Not to mention half New York.'

Suki looked across the crowded room to where the black head of Joel Harlow could just be seen at a quiet corner table. He was with a beautiful brunette in a flame-red dress and another couple who had just got up to dance. As Suki watched him, Joel Harlow glanced in her direction and their eyes tangled. He had a glass in his hand. He raised it slightly in a silent, unsmiling toast and she felt a curious electric prickle flash down her spine.

Hurriedly she looked away, her lashes fluttering against her flushed cheek. He bothered her. You couldn't call him handsome; his face was too powerful for that, but no doubt some women would describe him as strikingly attractive. He was disturbing, distinctly memorable, if you happened to like men who looked as if they could punch their way through a steel door. Suki did not fancy men like that. She could imagine that in an argument Joel Harlow always got his own way and that was a quality Suki felt should be steered clear of, if you were sensible.

'Watch him,' Rosie muttered at her side. 'I think he's got his eye on you, which could be difficult. He has the reputation of collecting beautiful women. He likes to have the best of everything, and that includes women. We don't want any trouble with him.'

'We won't have any,' said Suki. 'He may have his eye on me, but I don't fancy him.'

Rosie looked at her cynically. 'Darling, the man's loaded!'

'So what?'

'I don't just mean with money,' Rosie said. 'He has a lot of sex appeal, too.'

'Not for me.'

'Come off it,' Rosie said disbelievingly. 'All that machismo?'

'Doesn't turn me on.'

'I suppose that's just as well,' Rosie murmured, her face amused. 'He would be very distracting for you, just as your career is really hitting the heights.'

'What are you two whispering about?' Buddy demanded.

'You, sweetheart,' Rosie said, giving him a grin.

'Ah, my favourite subject,' Buddy purred, and Rosie watched him with indulgent amusement.

It was an hour later when Suki noticed Joel Harlow and his party leaving the club. She glanced after him, watching the oddly predatory lope of his long body. The floor was crowded with dancers now. Everyone was having a great time, enjoying themselves, and among that lighthearted crowd it should have been difficult to notice anyone at all, but Joel Harlow had more than one pair of female eyes riveted on him.

He turned as he was about to walk out of the door. Suki hadn't been expecting that and she was too late to look away. Their eyes met again, and again she felt that odd little reaction, her stomach plunging as though she was in a lift which had suddenly gone down without warning. He didn't smile, merely looked at her, yet she felt that brief glance as though it was a branding-iron, marking her out. He swung away and went, and Suki stared at the place where he had been, her eyes startled.

CHAPTER TWO

IT was almost dawn before they got back to the house and Suki was already asleep in the back of the car, her head against Rosie's shoulder, her slender body heavy with exhaustion.

'Sorry, baby, we've got to wake you,' said Buddy, shaking her, and she yawned, groaning before stumbling out of the car. Eyes almost shut, she walked into the bedroom and stripped before falling into bed, already asleep before she knew it.

Every so often she had a nightmare, a recurring nightmare she had had as long as she could remember. Nothing ever happened in it, no terrifying figures chased her, no danger threatened her, but all the same the dream always brought her screaming to a waking state, bolt upright in the bed.

Rosie burst into the room with Buddy behind her, their faces pale but unsurprised.

The light came on and they moved around the room, fetching a glass of water, talking comfortingly. It had happened too often before for them to ask any questions and, tonight of all nights, no doubt they had expected it.

It always happened either before or after an important performance; the stress of working in public always put her back into a past she preferred to forget.

She sipped the water, shivering, and Rosie stood by

the bed, a floating chiffon negligee flung over her night-dress, watching her while Buddy sat on the bed and patted her hand.

'Sorry,' she whispered.

'Forget it,' Buddy soothed, taking the glass from her trembling fingers. 'Okay now?'

She nodded and lay down again, very small and pale in the enormous bed, the fire of her hair emphasising the whiteness of her face. They said goodnight and went out, quietly closing the door, plunging the room back into darkness as they went. It had become a routine with them all. The dream was always the same and they had learnt to get her over it without talking about it. There was nothing anyone could say which would have any effect, they had discovered. The dream always came back as soon as she was under stress.

It underlay her vitality and life, the dancing electricity of her energy; a hidden flaw which, she sometimes felt, might actually feed the springs of that energy.

She stared into the darkness like a cat, her green eyes flickering, remembering with the waking mind what she had remembered in her sleep.

Turning over with a deep sigh, she pulled the continental quilt over her shoulders and went back to sleep, and this time she did not dream. When she woke up again it was to find the room filled with a blinding sunlight. It was late spring; the sky blue outside the window, the air fresh and crisp and alive with that special radiance only spring can give to the English landscape.

Rosie was putting a cup of tea down beside her, smiling. 'Photo-call at three o'clock, remember. Did you sleep again?'

'What time is it?' Suki was so sleepy she spoke in a thick, tired voice, and Rosie frowned.

'Almost noon. You look dead. Milly will be here soon. You're going to have to snap out of it before the press get here.'

Suki struggled up to sip her tea, eyelids drooping. She was in the state of weary depression which always followed a big creative effort. She had given out last night with everything she had, and now she was as flat as a pancake.

Rosie was glancing along the rows of dresses in the wall-to-wall wardrobe lining the room. Sunlight flashed back at Suki from the mirrors facing her. Rosie clicked her tongue and pulled out a black two-piece suit with orange flares zig-zagging across the loose blouson top. 'This will do,' she said, hooking it over the open wardrobe door.

'Okay,' Suki said obediently.

Rosie went out and Suki sat waiting for Milly, gazing blankly at her own reflection in the wall of mirrors, her body slender, vulnerable, childlike in the little cotton nightdress, the vivid blaze of her hair glittering in the sunlight. When she was not on public display she wore clothes she chose herself: jeans and sweaters and T-shirts, casual hard-wearing clothes in which she could be herself and forget the image Buddy and Rosie took so much care to build around her. The wardrobes full of highly expensive, daring clothes were part of her working equipment, part of the routine with which she built herself up to performing. She always allowed Rosie and Milly to decide what she should wear in public.

Milly bustled in ten minutes later. 'What's all this, then? Up you get and take a shower,' she scolded, and Suki slid out of the bed at once.

The house was a modern, white-painted building with four bedrooms, each with their own bathroom attached, the rooms spacious and luxuriously furnished, the house set back from a winding country road in Essex. A beautifully landscaped garden surrounded it and formed a buffer between the house and the outside world. Electrically operated iron gates kept out unwanted intruders and a high wall ran all the way round the grounds.

When they first moved into it, Suki had been overwhelmed by the place, but she had learnt that you can get used to anything in time. Now she took it for granted that she lived like this.

A middle-aged couple ran the house, keeping it in immaculate condition without ever making their presence felt. They lived in a small flat over the four-car garage at the side of the house. Rosie was not domesticated.

'If there's one thing I hate, it's housework,' she said frankly. 'Not to mention cooking—you've no sooner finished cooking a beautiful meal than along comes some pig and eats it.'

'Are you talking about me?' Buddy asked, and Rosie smiled angelically at him.

'If the cap fits . . .'

'You've got no creative spirit,' Buddy complained.

'Cooking isn't creative,' Rosie said. 'It's masochism. Why else would somebody spend hours making something for somebody else to wolf down in five minutes?'

Leaving Milly in the bedroom, Suki walked into the enormous bathroom and took a shower. The same evidence of luxury filled the bathroom; pale yellow fittings and trailing troughs of ferns giving the room a springlike air.

Milly eyed her pale face grimly a quarter of an hour later. 'I'm going to have to work my fingers to the bone getting you ready today, aren't I?' she commented. 'You look like something the cat brought in.'

'I feel like it.' Suki stared at herself in the mirror, seeing the bluish shadows under her slanting green eyes, the tired curve of her wide mouth, the tension in the tight pull of her skin across her cheekbones. 'I look terrible!'

'I told you to come straight home and get to bed.'

'I know you did.'

'Never take good advice, do you?'

'I was high last night.'

'And now you're right down,' Milly said gloomily.

'Little ray of comfort, where have you been all my life?' Buddy asked from the door, a tray in his hand.

'Hiding from you,' Milly snapped. 'Take a good look at her, will you? She doesn't need make-up—an injection of good red blood is what *she* needs, white as a ghost this morning. What did I say last night? She pushes herself too far and you let her, the pair of you. When did she last have a holiday?—and don't remind me that she had a week in Las Vegas before Christmas, that wasn't a holiday, it was purgatory. She worked herself to a standstill while she was there. She needs a long rest.'

Buddy put the tray down on the dressing table in front of Suki. 'Why don't we gag her?' he asked her in the mirror, his eyes meeting the reflection of hers. 'She drives me round the bend! I get all the nagging I need from Rosie.'

'Your wife's a saint,' Milly told him. 'What she puts up with nobody knows.'

'I'm going,' said Buddy, marching out.

Suki picked up the glass of ice-cold orange from the tray and sipped it, while Milly did her hair. She never ate breakfast. Her appetite was tiny, birdlike, a fact which was reflected in her slender figure.

The photographers arrived early. She saw them from the window as she sat casually on the windowsill, listening to Buddy outline the schedule for the next month. 'They're here,' she said, hearing the blare of a car horn, and Buddy went to press the button operating the electric gates.

The next hour was hectic as she posed around the house; in her bedroom sprawling on her bed, her chin propped in her hands, by the swimming pool, looking over one shoulder with a challenging, provocative expression, in the garden doing a high-flying leap like a ballet dancer, her smile dazzling. It was another form of performance and one she was used to, but it took more of that stored adrenalin and when the press had departed again she sank into a chair, groaning.

'That's me for the day,' she told Buddy.

He looked at Rosie and Suki stared from one to the other of them, a suspicious expression in her eyes.

'What now?' They were up to something, she knew that look. They had these little conspiracies from time to time, hiding things from her until they judged it safe to reveal whatever they were planning. She had been so young when they took her under their wing that they had fallen into the habit of treating her like a child.

'Look, baby,' Buddy began placatingly, and she linked her hands on top of her vivid head, bristling.

'What have you been cooking up for me now?'

Rosie fell to whistling under her breath, a sure indication that, for once, she was not entirely with Buddy in whatever he had up his sleeve.

'I got a phone call this morning,' Buddy said, that coaxing look on his thin face.

'Yes?'

'From Joel Harlow,' he added, unable to hide the excitement with which he announced that.

Suki sat up, stiffening. 'What did he want?' The very name had had a peculiar effect on her, and a wave of icy coldness trickled down her spine.

Rosie said bluntly: 'You—he wanted you.'

'He asked to speak to you,' Buddy interpreted hurriedly, glaring at his wife.

'But of course you were asleep,' Rosie pointed out.

'So I took the call,' Buddy said.

'And?' Suki had felt last night that that brief meeting was only a preliminary, one which Joel Harlow had intended as some sort of introduction to her but which he would follow up. He had left some sort of barbed hook in her, a strange frisson of alarm aroused deep inside her by the enigmatic scrutiny of those hard grey eyes. She wasn't surprised to hear he had followed up this morning.

Buddy opened his mouth, but Rosie beat him to it. 'He's coming to dinner tonight.'

'*What?*'

Buddy talked hurriedly, giving his wife a reproachful look. 'He was very impressed with you last night, baby, he wants to meet you and he could be a great help to us, you know. He could help build your career, especially in the States. He could do you a lot of good.'

'He's a shark,' Rosie said. 'A woman-eating shark.'

'He owns one of the biggest record companies in the States, and that means in the world,' Buddy snapped.

'He'll eat her alive, and guess who'll have to put the pieces together afterwards.'

'Suki has too much sense to get that involved with him,' Buddy said.

'Optimist!'

'All she has to do is play him nicely, flatter him and keep him interested,' Buddy said.

'She doesn't need him,' Rosie said firmly. 'Three years ago, maybe we could have done with his help, but not any more. Suki's big enough to get by without Joel Harlow, and he can only be dangerous to her.'

'What was I supposed to say to him? He's a very influential man, he can do us a lot of favours, but if we offend him he can also do us a lot of harm. If we box clever we can steer a middle course. I'm not suggesting Suki goes to bed with him.'

'Well, I'm glad about that,' Rosie said sarcastically. 'I was beginning to wonder.'

Suki sat in the chair listening to them patiently,

used to having them discuss her as if she was invisible, and her eyes moved from one to the other as they talked.

'He's coming to dinner, that's all,' Buddy muttered. 'Is that a crime? I had to be polite to him, didn't I?'

'Problems, nothing but problems,' sighed Rosie, grimacing. 'A pity he was in the nightclub last night and saw her. I had a funny feeling about that at the time.'

So did I, Suki thought, glancing at the expanse of blue sky she could see beyond the window, the tracery of budding branches moving softly against it as the wind quickened. A few clouds scudded before that wind, the weather was turning stormy—in more than one sense of the word, she told herself. Joel Harlow, was a man who made her feel tense and threatened, although she couldn't quite put her finger on why he should. He was not overtly menacing, but his face somehow conveyed the impression of a hidden mind which left no shred of evidence on the surface to warn you what was going on inside that black head.

There was silence. She looked round and found them both watching her, their faces oddly alike, concern in their eyes.

'All you have to do is be polite to him,' Buddy almost pleaded. 'We won't leave you alone with him.'

'And that's a promise,' said Rosie.

'Trust us?' Buddy asked, and Suki smiled at him with an effort, nodding.

'Louis's coming to dinner too,' Buddy told her, cheering up, his smile broad.

'With his new lady,' said Rosie, grinning. 'Geraldine, would you believe?'

'Geraldine?' repeated Suki, laughing.

'I can't wait to see her,' Rosie said, mischief in her eyes.

Louis Bax arranged all Suki's music, both for recording and for live shows. He was a clever, temperamental man in his late forties with a thin, clean-shaven face, a passion for good clothes and fast cars and a pair of shrewd, electric blue eyes. He was, in his way, a genius and had had a large part in building up Suki's career by choosing exactly the right songs for her. He had an ear for what would suit her voice and personality, and his temperament meant that if she argued with him about a song Louis was likely to go into a sulk which could last for weeks. He had known Buddy for twenty years, they were firm friends. Buddy's friends tended to stay friends and the approachable, wise-cracking temperament which made Buddy so popular had made his circle of friends grow steadily over the years. Buddy was always the one who coaxed Louis out of one of his sulks.

'Mr Fix-It will talk him round,' Rosie always said on one of these occasions, and it always worked. Buddy always came back smiling and the next day Louis was always back at work.

When Louis arrived that evening Suki was just pouring herself a glass of tomato juice while Buddy and Rosie sipped alcoholic drinks.

Louis came in, all smiles, with a girl in a short white mink jacket. She was tall and skinny and flat-chested with a head of tiny black curls framing a wooden face. Her eyes were elaborately made up with heavy glitter in a dark brown shade which made her look like a mournful panda. Louis talked and smiled and made jokes, but his companion didn't say a word.

The housekeeper, Mrs Morris, came in to whisk away the mink jacket and Geraldine asked coyly if she could visit the bathroom. While she was out of the room, Rosie asked Louis: 'What on earth do you see in *her*?'

'She's sexy,' Louis said.

'I'm speechless!' Rosie put a splayed hand over her face to prove it, gurgling.

'That'll be the day!' groaned Buddy.

'She hasn't got a word to say for herself,' said Rosie, and Louis looked complacent.

'That's what's so sexy about her. I never know what she's thinking. I like a lady who has an air of mystery.'

'That's not mystery, Louis, that's stupidity. She's not playing dumb—she *is* dumb.'

'It'll be fun finding out, though,' said Louis just as Geraldine returned to the room, the empty look pinned firmly to her face as they all looked at her. Two minutes later Joel Harlow was shown into the room and Suki felt herself tightening up inside, her stomach churning as though she was about to go on stage, his physical presence causing a chemical reaction in her which she couldn't quite understand. All she knew was that Joel Harlow threatened her, although why she should feel that she did not know. She had never felt like this before about any man.

Buddy bounced to meet him, smiling, but Suki sat rigidly on the dark blue velvet couch, her head lifted but her eyes not quite meeting the grey ones as Joel Harlow glanced across the room at her. She felt his gaze taking in the white chemise-style dress she wore, a tiny opaque bolero over it which matched it. The frilled old-fashioned look suited her, doused the brilliance of her red-gold hair and slanting sensuous green eyes, emphasised her youth and the vulnerable fragility of her fine-boned face. It had been designed for her and was one of her public appearance dresses. Rosie had told her to wear it tonight and she had unquestioningly obeyed.

'What will you have? Whisky?' Buddy lifted the decanter, eyeing Joel Harlow.

'Thank you,' he said, accepting the glass, then he turned and walked without haste but with every intention of choosing where he sat, to take the seat next to Suki. Nervously she looked sideways at him.

'Hallo,' he said in that deep smoky voice, sending a shiver down her spine.

'Hallo,' she said huskily.

Geraldine had been staring fixedly at Joel Harlow from the minute he walked into the room. She got up and slid across the room, sinuous as a snake, to take the seat on the other side of him.

'I saw you in a magazine,' she said, astonishing the others in the room. It was the first time she had said a syllable, and Rosie did a visible double-take.

Joel shifted slightly, turning his black head towards her. 'Really?' The courtesy was ice-cold and Suki wouldn't have liked to be on the receiving end of it.

Geraldine's face was almost lively. 'On your yacht in the Bahamas.'

He nodded without comment.

'Sailing,' Geraldine added, as though he might not have realised that.

'How fascinating,' Rosie murmured in honeyed tones, catching Suki's eye and giving her the shadow of a wink.

'How long are you staying in England?' Buddy asked him, and Joel Harlow said that he hadn't made up his mind. Suki looked down at her linked hands, twisting them into a new knot, playing cat's cradle with her slender fingers in a concentrated way. Out of the corner of her eye she could see the hard edge of his profile and her gaze drifted from that to his tanned hands, their sinewy strength at rest as he cupped his glass between them. He shifted and she felt his knee brush her own. It was a casual contact and he was talking to Buddy as it happened, but Suki moved away with a faint, suppressed intake of breath, and felt his glance shoot sideways at her.

'What do you think of the way the dollar's been yo-yoing?' Buddy asked him, and he shrugged.

'It was on the cards.'

There was a brief silence, then she felt him turning towards her and he said: 'Congratulations on getting your platinum disc. I read about it in the newspapers, last week.'

She smiled politely. 'Thank you.'

'She's got five golds as well, you know,' said Buddy, selling her hard, as usual. 'And she deserves them—she works at her career, Mr Harlow and she's a high-flyer, an achiever.' He leaned forward, excitement and insistence in his thin face. 'Some singers have everything else, a good voice, good stage presence, the lot, but they haven't got the drive and they never make it.'

Suki sat with her eyes lowered, biting the inside of

her lip. She was used to hearing herself talked about, but in Joel Harlow's sardonic presence it somehow jarred, it made her feel uneasy and on edge.

'You have to give it everything you've got,' Louis agreed, putting down his empty glass.

Joel Harlow lifted his own glass to his lips, listening as Buddy and Louis talked about her, the way they always did, with a sort of objective bluntness, ruthlessly analysing her faults as well as praising her, never sparing her feelings. It had stung, at first, hearing herself discussed so frankly. They showed her no mercy, but it was never unkind, merely honest, and she had learnt to listen and take note and try to improve on her weaknesses.

Absently she smoothed down the full white skirt of her dress, pleating it delicately with her slender fingers, and then stopped as she felt Joel Harlow's eyes on what she was doing. Her lashes fluttered, but she did not look round at him, a pinkness stealing into her face.

Over dinner Louis and Buddy got into a noisy wrangle over the arrangement of a new song and Suki listened, head lowered, faint amusement in her eyes.

'I tell you, she can't reach that note,' said Louis, waving a fork at Buddy.

'Who says?'

'I do. There isn't a thing about that voice I don't know,' Louis muttered.

Joel Harlow's grey eyes were fixed on Suki's face, she felt them probing coolly all the time and resented that unhidden speculation. Why doesn't he stop looking at me? she thought, prickling.

He leaned closer, his voice pitched too low for the others to pick up what he said.

'Do they always talk about you like that?'

Suki looked round, her lashes flickering up to leave the green slant of her eyes exposed to his stare, a slightly questioning look on her face.

'I'm sorry? How do you mean?'

His mouth had a sardonic twist as he went on: 'I picked it up last night in that club and I've seen it again tonight—they talk about you as if you had no say in yourself at all. You're their possession, their child, their puppet—you don't belong to yourself, you belong to them.'

'Buddy's my manager, he's built my whole career,' she retorted, frowning. 'I owe him everything I've got, him and Rosie.'

'And in return, you let them run your life?'

She didn't answer.

'You live here with them, don't you?'

Suki nodded, eyes lowered.

'What about your family? How do they see that?'

She froze, her whole face tightening, and didn't say a word.

He waited a moment and when it was apparent that she had no intention of answering the question asked another. 'How old are you?'

'Twenty-two,' she said. That was an easy question to answer, and anyway, he could find that out just by asking Buddy.

There was a silence from him. She glanced at him and met his eyes. 'And how long have you been part of this circus?' he asked.

'Five years.'

His brows arched sharply. 'Five years? Since you were . . .'

'Seventeen,' she prompted.

'How did you come to get involved with them?'

'Buddy found me, he discovered me.'

'How?'

Suki looked away, her pale throat moving in a swallow of nervous reluctance. She did not want to tell him too much about herself, she did not want him to know too much about her.

'Where were you born?' he asked. 'Are you a Londoner?'

Suki glanced at Rosie, her green eyes beseeching, and Rosie leaned over in response to say: 'You're something of an expert on wine, I gather, Mr Harlow? What do you think of this one?'

He turned that way, a cold impatience in the tautness of his jaw, but he answered with remote courtesy. 'Excellent. I'm enjoying it very much.'

'Where are you staying in London?' Buddy asked, and Suki saw Joel Harlow's hand close into a hard fist on the table as he answered.

'My company owns a penthouse suite in the new block of flats at the edge of the park in Mayfair.'

'You must have a great view from there,' Rosie said with warm enthusiasm.

'I do,' he said with that cool politeness. Suki's green eyes flicked up and met Rosie's. There was wry amusement in Rosie's glance. Buddy asked the next question and Joel Harlow replied with the restrained impatience which his tough features underlined. He knew what they were doing, he knew they were constantly distracting him from Suki, keeping him otherwise occupied, and he didn't like it, but his habit of good manners prevented him from ignoring them.

They took their coffee in the long lounge and Rosie deliberately sat down next to Suki before Joel Harlow could reach the seat. His grey eyes observed them coolly while he drank his coffee, listening to Buddy. He placed his empty cup on the low coffee table and turned towards Suki, extending a lean, tanned hand.

'I'd like to see your gold discs.' That hand closed round her wrist and jerked her to her feet before she could think of an excuse. 'Where are they?'

'In my office,' said Buddy, jumping to his feet. 'I'll be glad to show them to you.'

At that moment the telephone rang, and after a moment's hesitation Rosie got up and went to answer it, her long skirts rustling as she walked across the room. She gave Buddy a warning look as she passed him and he grinned cheerfully at Joel Harlow.

'We're very proud of our star, Mr Harlow. She's come a long way in a short time and she's going further, she's going right to the very top. One day we'll have gold discs wall-to-wall, won't we, Louis?'

'Sure,' Louis agreed.

Geraldine gave a wail, staring at one of her hands. 'I've broken a nail!'

Louis swung round as she extended a trembling hand to him, brokenhearted horror in her face. 'That's tragic, sugar,' he said, taking her hand and kissing it. One of the long, perfectly manicured nails had torn and was hanging loose, ruining the whole effect.

'Good grief!' Buddy muttered.

Rosie swung excitedly, holding out the phone. 'New York, Buddy, they want to talk to *you*.'

He rushed over there and began to talk with explosive energy while Rosie stood close to him, trying to hear what was being said at the other end.

Joel Harlow looked down at Suki, a gleam in his grey eyes. His hand began to push her towards the door and she glanced up at him warily. Before she could think of an excuse to delay, he was steering her into Buddy's office next door and closing the door. She was relieved when he released her, his eye falling on the row of gold discs behind Buddy's desk. He strolled over there and studied them while Suki hovered, biting her lip.

He swivelled, the grey eyes travelling over her as he spoke. 'Very impressive.'

'Thank you.'

'You've come a very long way in the last couple of years, I gather.'

She nodded. 'Thanks to Buddy and Rosie.'

His mouth indented wryly. 'Ah, yes.' There was a pause, then he said in a rapid voice: 'You're a contradiction, do you know that? I can't make you out. You've hardly said a word all evening and in that dress you look like a shy schoolgirl.' He flicked another glance over it, the hard eyes making it clear that he did not appreciate the demure, sweet style. 'Where's the girl I saw last night, dancing around like a living flame? When you walked on stage in that black dress you came over the footlights as the sexiest lady I've ever seen. You took my breath away.'

Her cheeks burnt and her eyes lowered, but she

didn't answer him. He watched her, waiting, then said: 'Tonight you're covered up from head to foot like a nun and you've got about as much sparkle as flat champagne.'

'Sorry,' Suki said, her temper rising as she listened, and her voice snapped like a lash.

'Which is the real Suki Black?' he asked, and she shrugged her slender shoulders, her smile cold.

'I'm probably the last person in the world who could tell you that. We never know ourselves, do we?'

'Most of us have got a clue,' he said drily. 'At least, by the time we become adults we have some idea about ourselves. I've heard a lot tonight from your manager and his wife, but I've barely got a whisper out of you and I haven't been able to get an idea what you're really like.'

She glanced at him and away. 'You'll have to make up your own mind about that.'

'Have dinner with me and give me the chance to find out.'

She stiffened. 'I'm sorry——' she began, but he cut her short before she could come up with an excuse.

'I won't take no for an answer, I never do. Like you, I know what I want and I go for it and never accept a refusal.' He smiled at her as he said that, charming mockery in his face, and Suki lifted her chin, her back rigid with determination.

'In this case, I'm afraid you're going to have to accept a refusal, Mr Harlow. I'm very busy and my career leaves me no time for much of a private life.'

His face tightened, the charm vanishing. Staring at

her, he said: 'No room for a private life? I presume that means men?'

She didn't answer, looking at him levelly.

'No love affairs?' There was a sharpness in his voice now, and she reacted to the tone by lifting one brow coldly, her green eyes freezing over.

He pushed his hands into his pockets, rocking backwards and forwards on his heels, his black head tilted back slightly as he surveyed her, his lids half lowered as if to hide what he was thinking, the grey eyes gleaming unreadably through the thick battery of long lashes. Suki found herself staring back at him and thinking that he had the most unforgettable eyes she had ever seen, their shape and colour unique and extraordinary. In that tough, masculine face they were oddly out of place, their beauty contradicting the hardness of the bone structure, the coldness of the strong mouth.

'How long has this been going on?' he demanded. 'Haven't you ever had any men friends?'

A flush ran up her face and she couldn't control the startled gasp which came out of her. She had been so stupidly intent on watching those amazing eyes of his that she had forgotten everything else. She didn't answer, but her silence apparently spoke for her.

'Is this state of affairs their idea?' He jerked his head towards the door.

'Of course not!'

'But they do run your whole life, don't they?'

She resented the way he put that, the implication that Buddy and Rosie manipulated her, took advantage of her. She owed them everything, and she wasn't going to have a total stranger walking in and attacking them without knowing anything about the set-up.

'Of course they don't! Don't be ridiculous.'

'No?' His black brows curved in sardonic query.

'You just don't understand!'

'Then explain it to me.'

'They're my family!' That was what they were, how she always thought of them. They were her family, the only family she had, had ever had, and they were the first people in the world with whom she had ever felt she belonged, with whom she had ever felt safe and at ease.

Joel Harlow watched the excited anger in her face, his eyes narrowed. 'They really have you under lock and key, don't they? They own you body and soul.'

'That's nonsense!'

'Is it? Why do you put up with it? Why let them run your life and dictate everything you do, everywhere you go, everything you wear or sing?'

She moved restlessly, a glowing anger deep in the deep eyes. 'They have to run things, take decisions for me. If I don't agree, they always listen and discuss their reasons, tell me why things have to be done that way.'

He laughed tersely. 'My God, you can't be for real! And you swallow that? Can't you see that you're just their puppet? Of course they don't want you to get involved with anyone else, have any love affairs. That might ruin things for them. I can see their side of it— but you, why do you just accept it? Are you frigid?'

Her skin was burning hot, her green eyes glimmering with rage, but she didn't answer and he watched her intently, then said in a slow voice: 'But I haven't got that right, have I? You *do* have a love affair.'

Suki still said nothing, staring at him with hostility.

'You have a million of them, don't you?' he murmured, his mouth twisting. 'A million lovers every time you walk on to a stage. That's why you were practically on fire last night. Your only love affair is with your audience, and no real man could compete with them.'

She was bitterly angry at the expression on his face, the dry note in his voice, and she moved towards the door, intent on escape. He crossed the room at the same moment to cut her off and she felt a flare of terror, her face paling as his hand shot out to stop her. She stopped in her tracks, rigid, and he moved closer, speaking softly against her vivid hair, his lean body brushing hers.

'It's time you came out of that dream world and found out what you're missing,' he murmured. 'Have dinner with me tomorrow. I want to get to know you, find out what you're really like.'

'No,' she said unsteadily, a pulse beating at the base of her white throat.

'Why not?' he curved a long-fingered hand round her throat, turning her face towards him, and she looked up with frightened green eyes, her lips quivering, her face very pale.

She nerved herself, fear making her courage come back. 'Why should you think you have the right to know anything except what I choose to tell you?'

'Why are you so secretive? What have you got to hide?' he demanded, staring down into her eyes, the black pupils of his own eyes enlarged and brilliant.

'Let go of me,' she retorted. 'I haven't got anything

to hide, don't be absurd!'

'Then why are you so jittery at the idea of me knowing anything about you?'

'I'm not jittery!'

His brows curved derisively. 'I'd say you were, you look like someone in the last stages of a fit of panic. Why do you hate answering questions about yourself? I had someone do some research on you, hunt through some newspaper clippings, but surprisingly little came up. You're very secretive. Why?'

'I tell people what I feel like telling them,' Suki said angrily. 'We all have a right to the privacy of our own heads. People are always trying to nail you down, label you, catalogue you as though you were some sort of insect. Well, nobody has the right to put someone else into a catalogue, Mr Harlow, and nobody is doing that to me!'

'That's more like it,' he said in a satisfied tone, and moved his hand caressingly up her throat.

Suki gasped and jerked her head back, protesting. 'Don't!'

'Keep talking to me,' he said, smiling down at her with lazy, interested eyes. 'That sounded like the girl I saw on stage, singing with all that passion—that's the girl I want to see again.'

Her eyes flickered in nervous impatience. 'Would you kindly let go of me? I don't want to talk to you.'

'Why not?' he demanded. 'Can't you commit yourself to a real relationship, is that it? Do you prefer fantasy, Suki?'

'Don't be so damned insulting,' she spluttered, pushing him away and swinging towards the door. She didn't get very far. She felt his hands close on her slender waist and swivel her back towards him, controlling her as effortlessly as though she was a child. Suki glared at him, face burning with temper by now, her green eyes brilliant with rage.

'I've got it, haven't I?' Joel Harlow said mockingly. 'No one-to-one relationship could match up to the fantasy you live in—from out front the audience can't see the real Suki, can they? All they see is the star, the glittering dancing star, and that's what you want them to see, isn't it? You prefer the illusion to reality and so do they, those people out in the dark watching you.'

She struggled in his hands, twisting from side to side, burning with helpless fury, impotent and forced to listen. He lifted one powerful hand and cupped her chin, lifting it so that she had to look at him.

'Isn't it cold, trapped inside a fantasy world, Suki?' he asked, in that smoky, mocking voice and her rage almost hit the top of her head, spurring her to a final, violent struggle which released her for a moment. She took the opportunity to flee, muttering: 'Goodbye!' as she pulled open the door.

'I'm never saying goodbye to you, Suki,' Joel Harlow said softly, and she slammed the door on his words, trembling as she ran towards her own bedroom.

CHAPTER THREE

She was in bed half an hour later when Rosie tapped and came into the room, glancing at her quickly, trying to read her expression. She wandered over and sat down on the edge of the bed, lacing her hands around her knee.

'He's gone.'

Suki was reading a magazine, her mind having a struggle to stay on the glossy pages. She kept her eyes on a fashion picture, her brows level.

'What happened?' Rosie asked, watching her.

'Nothing. He looked at the discs and asked a few questions.' She was oddly reluctant to tell Rosie what he had said. It was still rankling, lingering at the back of her mind, raising questions she preferred not to face.

'Sorry we fell down on keeping him away from you,' said Rosie, her voice wry. 'That was an exciting call—it looks as if a tour of the States is a certainty for next year.' She sparkled as she said that. 'Nothing's settled yet, but I'd say it is going to come off.'

'That's great,' said Suki. A week ago she would have been leaping with excitement but, oddly, tonight she felt dull, and, of course, Rosie picked that up at once.

'Aren't you thrilled?' She sounded scandalised. Rosie was excited, she was bubbling with it. She couldn't

understand why Suki reacted with such quiet acceptance. Rosie had already forgotten Joel Harlow. The
telephone call from New York had erased him from
her mind, and although she had spoken briefly about
the moments when he got Suki alone, she wasn't
really either interested or concerned.

'Of course I am,' said Suki, smiling, closing the
magazine.

'This is what we've been working for—if you're to
be a world star you have to go over big in the States.'

'I know.' She had had that drummed into her over
and over again in the last five years.

'You look as excited as someone who just got handed
a sandwich when they were expecting caviar,' Rosie
said disapprovingly. She got up, brushing down her
full skirts. 'You're tired. You'd better get a good
night's sleep. Rehearsal tomorrow in the studio, remember.'

Suki put the magazine on her bedside table and lay
down, her cheek curled on her hand. Rosie walked towards the door and flicked off the light.

'Are we pushing you too hard, Suki?' she asked
quietly in the dark. 'Are you feeling the pace these
days?'

'Of course not,' Suki said at once.

Rosie was silent. 'Maybe you ought to have a holiday,'
she mused, almost to herself. 'Maybe Milly's right.'

'Milly's a killjoy, she just talks for the sound of it.'

'All the same, she could have something,' said Rosie,
then she went out and closed the door.

Suki lay in the bed, struggling to relax, trying to evict
Joel Harlow from his possession of her mind, but un-

able to forget the feel of that strong yet oddly gentle hand on her throat. She put her own hand there as if he had left marks which she could trace, her fingers trembling. It was a long time since any man had got close enough to touch her like that. She had walled herself behind glass, a transparent wall between her and the world, and tonight Joel Harlow had broken through that invisible barrier to lay his hand on her.

She turned over in the bed heavily, biting her lip, burying her face in the pillows.

She had known he was dangerous the moment she met his eyes in that nightclub. Most men she met were shadowy figures on the far side of that wall of hers, moving around her and never coming close enough to make her aware of them, but with that first brief contact of the eyes Joel Harlow had made an impact on her that had disturbed her. For five years she had been engrossed in the remote dream of stardom and fame which Buddy had held out to her and she had needed nothing else. When she stood on that stage she was alive and locked in a passionate exchange with the people out in the audience, moving with them on the heights of a wild elation born of the music. Recording in a studio could never give her what live performances gave her. She needed the fix those moments held. She was hooked on the sound of those voices out there, the feel of their involvement with her.

Joel Harlow hadn't told her anything she didn't know, even though she had denied it to him.

He had been trying to make her admit it, but why should she? Why should she tell him anything, admit anything? She didn't want him too close. She didn't want him to know her, it threatened the security of her invisible force-field. If she once let anyone through, the world might flood in and drown her. She was only safe while she was alone in her head, her only moments of release while she was on stage and letting the submerged passion flow out towards the unseen faces. It all built up in her in between performances, an intense emotion which crashed out when she began to sing.

Outside the house the wind blew through the elm trees along the far corner of the garden and Suki listened to them blankly, her mind obsessed. She fell asleep at last, worn out by her struggle with herself, and at some time in the night she woke up with a gasp from the dream. It was rare for her to dream it two nights running, and this time she hadn't screamed out. The room was silent and she hadn't disturbed Rosie and Buddy. She lay, shuddering, her inward eye still fixed on the grey emptiness the dream held.

She hated waking up from it in the room alone. Loneliness was the worst thing life could offer. She lay tense and still in the bed, then switched on the light. It was a relief to sit up in the blaze of brightness, a relief to lean over and turn on the radio and tune in to some late-night music show, hear the chat of the disc jockey as he filled in between discs. Suki listened but did not hear much of what he was saying, then a wry smile touched her lips as a familiar sound throbbed out. Her own voice still sounded odd to her. She turned the radio off again, switched out the light and lay down to sleep again.

She was just finishing her morning orange juice when Rosie came in carrying a large box. Suki raised her brows as Rosie flipped off the lid to reveal several dozen perfect dark red roses.

'Guess who,' said Rosie, grinning.

Suki felt a faint pink steal into her face and was annoyed with herself. 'Who?' she asked, pretending she had no idea.

Rosie wasn't deceived. She gave her a wry look and plucked the card out of the box, tossing it to her.

There was no message, just the name scrawled in powerful black handwriting.

'Joel Harlow,' Suki said aloud.

'Surprise, surprise.' Rosie peeled back the cellophane covering and took out one long-stemmed flower, raising it to her face. 'Roses have such a marvellous scent, don't they?' She held it towards Suki, who breathed in the delicate fragrance.

'Lovely!'

Rosie dropped the flower back into the box, surveying her with dry amusement.

'What are you going to do about him?'

'I'm not going to do anything.'

'He's in pursuit, you know that.'

'I'm not interested,' Suki shrugged. 'He'll get the message eventually.'

'Let's hope so,' Rosie murmured, biting her little finger. 'But I don't feel so sure, myself. He looks to me like a man who's used to getting what he wants. The list of his women reads like a mini version of *Who's Who*—he always chooses fabulous ladies, those from his own world. He likes his women to be rich and famous in their own right. He's a collector.'

'Well, he isn't collecting me!'

'You're so strong-minded,' Rosie said sarcastically. 'Now, me, if he was giving me a strong come-on I wouldn't have the willpower to say no.'

Suki laughed. 'You know you would. You wouldn't want to break Buddy's heart.'

'What heart?' Rosie asked, going to the door. Milly came into the room as she went out and threw Suki a scolding look.

'Aren't you up yet?'

'Yes,' said Suki, taking a flying leap out of the bed and making her way to the bathroom.

Buddy drove her to the rehearsal studio, dropped her there and went off to his office, saying: 'I'll be back at one to pick you up.'

Louis was in the control room talking to several other men. He waved to Suki as she wandered into the studio, a slender figure in smoothly fitting jeans and a white T-shirt, a chunky black knitted jacket over the top which she kept on for a while as she started work.

It was a slow, monotonous process, constantly interrupted by Bill Winter, the producer, who kept flicking down his mike and leaning forward to stop her and make some comment, ask her to change something, do it a different way. Suki sat on a high stool in the centre of the studio with the mike in front of her, headphones clamped over her ears. The group were behind her, out of sight, but now and then she looked over her shoulder and grinned at them, getting back smiles.

At last Bill seemed satisfied. 'Break for coffee,' he said in her ear, and she climbed off the stool, taking off the headphones and hanging them over the leather seat. It was stuffy and overheated in the control room, the air full of smoke. The group crowded in with her, talking about a football game, and Suki took her paper cup of coffee and wandered off with it into the corridor. She stood by a window staring at the windy sky, her mind on what she had just been doing.

When a pair of hands closed over her arms she jumped, glancing round in shock.

'Hallo,' said the deep, husky voice she was beginning to know.

She looked into the mocking grey eyes and then away again, her pulses beginning to quicken. 'What are you doing here?'

'I came along to eavesdrop.'

Her brows met. 'How did you know I was here?'

'I rang your manager and his secretary told me.'

'Oh, did she?' Suki made a mental note to tell Buddy that the girl had been indiscreet enough to blurt that out. It could have been anyone ringing up to enquire about her whereabouts. The press could have descended in a tidal wave on the studio. It wasn't unknown for fans to ring up and ask where she could be found—the surprising thing was that Buddy's secretary had been stupid enough to actually tell Joel Harlow where she was, she should have known better.

'Don't blame her,' he said, watching Suki shrewdly. 'I told her who I was.'

Suki gave him an ironic glance. 'And that unlocked her tongue, did it?'

He smiled. 'I do have some pull.'

'You do,' she agreed. And he wouldn't hesitate to use it, she recognised, eyeing him.

'I'm glad you realise that,' he said, a faintly teasing

note in his voice. He smiled down into her eyes, charm in his face, and her eyes wavered before they lowered. As they dropped she was unwillingly absorbing how he looked today. Dressed as casually as she was, he wore a smooth black silk shirt, the collar open, the tailored fit of it emphasising that lean build, with a pair of figure-hugging black jeans which made him look taller than ever. A white suede jacket was slung around his shoulders and she shivered with angry reaction as she stared at her feet, not wanting to be aware of that male attraction but unable to hide from herself that she was conscious of it.

He took off the jacket and put it round her own shoulders, his hands holding the collar so that it framed her startled face as she looked up.

'Cold?' he asked softly. 'You're pale, you work too hard. Isn't it time you slowed down a bit, Miss Suki Black?'

Her lashes fluttered against her cheek. She felt the warm brush of his fingers against her cheek and knew he was smiling.

'Have lunch with me.'

She shook her head. 'I'm having lunch with Buddy.'

'He won't miss you.'

She found herself smiling unwillingly at the teasing voice. 'He would, I'm afraid.'

'Hey, Suki!'

She looked over her shoulder at Bill Winter who stood in the doorway, staring at them curiously.

'We're ready for you,' Bill said, and she nodded.

'Okay, I'm coming.'

Bill gave Joel Harlow a look, then went back into the

studio. Suki took off the suede jacket, her fingers lingering with appreciation on the smooth soft skin, then handed it back to Joel.

'Thank you,' she said gravely, turning away. He stood watching her as she walked back into the studio without a pause, and although she did not look back she knew his eyes stayed fixed on her every step of the way, the hair on the back of her neck stirring in nervous response.

Now that she was actually going to record she stayed on her feet, using full power, her body swaying with the beat. She heard Bill's soft whistle of appreciation when they finished the first take and through the glass he gave her a thumbs-up which she returned, smiling.

It was another hour before he was satisfied he had enough and Suki was weary, one hand massaging her spine as she walked to the door.

'Drink, Suki?' Bill asked as she looked in at the others. He had a bottle of whisky in one hand and the rest of them were already drinking out of paper cups. Suki glanced at her watch and shook her head, sliding into her knitted jacket.

'Buddy's picking me up in one minute.' She raised a hand to them all. 'Lovely music, thanks, I enjoyed it.'

They all raised their cups, grinning, than went back to their noisy dissection of what had gone wrong on the second take.

When she stepped out into the chill spring air, the sun had just been swallowed up in cloud and she shivered, glancing up at the sky. It floated out again, pale fragments of mist trailing after it, and Suki half-shut her eyes, enjoying the warmth of the sunlight as it touched her face. She heard the car purr smoothly to a halt beside her. The door opened and she slid, smiling, into the passenger seat, slamming the door as she turned to look at Buddy.

It wasn't Buddy. For a second she didn't move, her eyes wide in shock as she looked into those grey eyes, then she turned and tried to scramble out again, but he had already put the car into motion and was shooting away from the kerb in a burst of speed.

'What do you think you're doing?' Suki asked in raw anger, her hand fumbling with the door catch. 'Stop the car at once!'

He took no notice and she bit her lower lip, frowning, looking back towards the entrance to the studios, her face pale.

'Buddy will wonder what on earth has happened to me!'

'Let him wonder.' Joel Harlow was totally impervious to such a suggestion, his broad shoulders shrugging indifferently as he spoke, and she stared at him impotently.

'You can't do this!'

'Just watch me.' That seemed to amuse him, he was smiling as he answered.

The sleek black limousine was streaking away and they were out of sight of the studios now.

They halted at some traffic lights and she hurriedly caught hold of the door handle again, pressing it down. The door stayed shut.

'It's electronically controlled from the dashboard,' Joel Harlow informed her.

She flung round to face him, screwed up inside with

rage and impotent resentment. 'You can't just kidnap me like this! Can't you get it through your head? I don't want to know!'

His black lashes flicked sideways and a wry smile touched his mouth. 'I did gather that, yes.'

'Then why . . .'

'There's only one thing to do when you meet sales resistance,' he said mockingly. 'Beat it down. You don't know the first thing about me. It isn't me you're turning down—it's any sort of involvement with any-one, isn't it?' The lights turned green and he set the car moving again, talking with his eyes on the road ahead. 'I'm not giving up in those circumstances. You may be packed in ice, but let's see what effect a little heat will have.'

She sat stiffly in the seat, her hands curled into little balls. 'You've got a nerve!'

He laughed softly, shooting her a quick smile. 'Just sit still and enjoy the scenery.'

'I'm not going to enjoy anything.'

'We'll see about that.'

The calm words sent a trail of ice down her spine. She looked at him through her lashes. The hard-edged profile had no hint of a flaw, there was no crack in the wall of his determination to get his own way.

She sank back into the seat, watching as he mani-pulated the steering wheel between those long, firm fingers.

'Where are you taking me?'

'It's a surprise.'

'You can say that again,' she muttered, and he laughed under his breath again.

'When you get to know me better . . .'

'If I do,' Suki said, and he gave her another of those flicking, mocking smiles.

'When you do,' he insisted. 'You'll realise that if I set my mind to get something, I get it.'

She sat upright, very tense, her red-gold head gleaming in the sunlight, her green eyes glowing with anger. 'Even Napoleon met his Waterloo.'

'You are not going to be my Waterloo, Suki,' Joel Harlow said smoothly as he edged his way through the heavy north-bound traffic. 'At this moment, I don't know what you're going to be—which makes it very intriguing. You're a challenge, and I enjoy challenges. Nothing is exciting if you get it too easily.'

'You're not getting me,' Suki muttered. 'Easily or otherwise.' She was desperately searching for some way of escape, but while they were in this car with those doors locked she couldn't think of anything which wouldn't cause a scandal, something she wanted even less than she wanted to spend a few hours with Joel Harlow. His intentions couldn't be a serious threat to her, but all the same she didn't want to be alone with him for any length of time. He unnerved her.

'Do you like the country?' he asked as they made their way through the grim streets of the northern suburbs.

She didn't answer, staring out of the window and ignoring him. He glanced at her, took one hand off the wheel and ran his fingers along her thigh in a caressing, intimate gesture to which she reacted with bitter fury, slapping his hand away and shrinking back in her seat, her eyes hating him.

'Keep your hands off me!'

'Answer me, then, stop sulking,' he said coolly.

Suki stared at him and he smiled drily.

'When you take on a battle, Suki, always make sure your weapons are up to it. I'm stronger than you are and you aren't getting away from me for a while, so come out of your shell and try being pleasant to me for once.'

She didn't answer; her face was very pale. She could still feel the trail of his fingers on her jean-clad leg, and her nervous apprehension had grown with that deliberate invasion.

'Have you always lived in London?' he asked casually, giving her one brief glance.

'Yes.' She answered without thinking, her voice husky.

'Where do your family live?'

'I haven't got one.'

She felt him looking at her again, but she didn't meet his eyes. 'No parents living now?'

She shook her head.

'What happened?'

Suki evaded that question and, to distract him, asked one in turn. 'What about you? Are your parents alive?'

'My father died ten years ago, but my mother's still going strong.' He smiled, a wry tenderness in the curve of his mouth which changed his whole face. 'She's seventy this year, but she pilots her own plane and is fanatical about her racing stable. I often think that that's what keeps her mind so young. She's so busy with her plans for each racing season that she hasn't noticed how old she's getting.'

Suki found herself laughing. 'Have you got any brothers and sisters?'

'Two sisters,' he said. 'Have you?'

Her smile vanished. 'No.' She looked away. 'Are your sisters married?'

He nodded. 'They live in the States. Julie has got two children, both boys, and Lee has got a baby girl. My mother's a very proud grandparent.'

'But you've never married?' That was surprising, Suki thought, watching him. His profile tightened and he glanced at her, not smiling.

'Yes, I was married once.'

She felt a jolt of surprise. 'You're divorced?'

'She died.' He was heading out of the suburbs now and into the green countryside on the northern edge of London. He stared ahead, his brows straight and his mouth hard. 'It was a long time ago.'

'An accident?' Suki asked.

'She died in childbirth,' Joel said curtly, and Suki winced.

'I'm sorry.'

He nodded without glancing at her.

'The baby?' she asked in a low, husky voice.

'Died too.' There was a harsh note in his voice and she didn't like to say anything after that for a while. He drove with his gaze fixed on the road, a brooding darkness in his face. What had his wife been like? she wondered. Had he loved her very deeply? Obviously the subject still had the power to hurt him. He hadn't got over it yet. How long ago had it happened?

'Have you always wanted to be a singer?' he asked, making her jump because she had been so intent on her own thoughts that she hadn't noticed anything else for sometime.

Suki relaxed slightly, the thick lashes sweeping back from her slanting green eyes as she smiled. 'As long as I can remember.' She gave a deep sigh. 'I waited a long, long time to get where I am. It seemed like forever at times. You can't even be sure you're going to make it, you can only keep on going, trying, hoping that this time you'll break through.' She had almost forgotten who she was talking to, her mind absorbed in the past and so altered by hearing about his dead wife and the baby that had never lived that her hostility to him had taken a new turn and become a sort of guarded acceptance.

'How did you meet your manager?'

'I was singing in a pub with a group of semi-amateurs. Buddy heard me and decided he liked the way I sang.' She laughed. 'I thought I was pretty good myself, then. I was so green I didn't know how bad I was.'

Joel smiled. 'But you had star quality and he spotted it?'

'I had something, I suppose,' she said frankly. 'I was very ragged and my timing was way off, but I could belt songs out even then.'

'How old were you?'

'Seventeen.'

'What did your parents think about your dream of getting into the pop world?'

Her body stiffened. 'They didn't get asked.'

She felt his quick look. 'You didn't just leave home without a word?'

'Home?' Suki laughed harshly, her skin white with pain and her green eyes burning between those long lashes. 'I never had a home, Mr Harlow, or any parents.

I haven't even got a name. I was found in the street. I was a few hours old, wrapped in a blanket, and nobody ever came forward to claim me.'

There was silence as the car purred along between high thick-set hedges, the sky overhead a cloudy pale blue, on either side fields stretching away into a misty distance. Suki was trembling, her body tight as a coiled spring. She hated talking about it, hated remembering the years before she met Buddy. Every time she thought about her own beginnings she felt sick.

'That was tough,' Joel said gently, and she hated him for that quiet voice because how could he possibly know what it felt like to be her, to know that you had been rejected right at the beginning of your life, dumped ruthlessly in the street and left to die. It had been a cold, rainy winter night and it had been a miracle she lived. She knew that because they had told her so at the children's home. They had gone on about that, because they wanted her to thank God for her miraculous preservation. She might have escaped notice until morning, by which time she would have been dead of exposure, if it hadn't been for the fact that somebody's dog had heard her weak mewing and come to investigate. His barking had alerted his owner and saved her life. Suki hadn't been able to feel much gratitude towards that divine intervention at the time. She had been too busy hating whoever had dumped her.

She turned and looked at Joel Harlow. 'You see, we haven't got a thing in common, Mr Harlow. You know who you are, where you come from—you belong, you're sure of your identity. I don't know anything about myself.'

He pulled over to the side of the road and parked at the edge of a small copse. Suki sat stiffly in her seat, her face rigid.

'Why have you parked?'

He didn't answer, but slid a hand into the inside pocket of his suede jacket. She watched as he brought out a slim gold case, opened it and took out a long cheroot. He flicked a button on the dashboard and his window slid silently down. Joel leaned forward and took the cigar lighter from the dashboard. Suki watched as he lit his cheroot, replacing the lighter deftly before leaning back in his seat, the blue smoke beginning to float away out of the car as he exhaled.

Taking the cigar out of his mouth, he gazed thoughtfully at the glowing tip of it. 'You know as much about yourself as any of us do, Suki.'

She laughed angrily. 'What would you know about it? I come from a very different world from you, Mr Harlow. You couldn't introduce someone like me to your friends, or your family—the minute they asked me who I was, where I sprang from, a nasty big hole would open up. People like to have a way of placing you, pigeonholing you, particularly rich people like the people you come from.'

'What a little snob you are,' he murmured softly, and her face burnt with furious colour.

'Don't be ridiculous! What would I have to be snobbish about?'

'What would I?' he asked, his grey eyes flickering towards her, mocking amusement in them.

Suki's teeth met and she said through them: 'You don't need to be, do you?'

'And you do?'

'I didn't say that! Don't twist my words.'

'I'm merely trying to interpret them,' he told her calmly with that shrewd sideways look. The car had filled with the aromatic scent of the cheroot. She watched him gently tip a coil of grey ash into the ashtray, his gaze unreadable.

'Is this why you cut yourself off from any real relationships?' he asked.

'I have plenty of real relationships! I have dozens of friends, but they're all people from my own world, musicians and singers. They're the sort of people who don't ask questions all the time, who accept you for what you are.'

'Then you do know who you are,' he said, and she paused, lips parted in impatience as their eyes met.

'You're Suki Black, one of the top singing stars in this country,' he told her gently. 'You're sexy and beautiful and very talented, and who your parents were, or where you come from, doesn't matter a damn to anybody.'

She laughed bitterly. 'Doesn't it? Then why was it that you started asking me questions? We've only just met and you knew I was Suki Black and you knew I was a singer, but you had to know more than that, didn't you? You started probing, questioning, trying to find out all about me. You were trying to place me, catalogue me.'

Joel flung his cheroot out of the window with an abrupt gesture and turned towards her. 'I was trying to make some sort of contact with you, understand you,' he told her grimly. 'I wanted to know why you were so frozen up inside and I thought I could get through to you by going slowly, getting to know you. I can see I chose the wrong approach.'

'I don't want an approach of any kind!' Suki flung back at him.

'You made that very clear.'

'Then why don't you get the message? Turn this car round and take me back to where I belong and in future stay away from me.'

The grey eyes held her own, his pupils enlarged and glittering, his breathing audible in the quiet country lane. Suki felt a dart of cold warning, then his hands clamped her arms and his head swooped down towards her. It happened too fast for her to have a chance of evading him. The harsh, bruising pressure of his mouth took her by surprise and her lips parted in a stifled protest.

Joel shifted, and his hands slipped round her, lifting her closer, his demanding kiss inescapable. Suki put her hands against his chest, pushing him away without having any effect. The lean, muscled body was immovable and her fingers curled impotently into his shirt. The shaking grew inside her, her body trembling violently in the hard circle of his arms.

She could feel the warm movements of his hand fondling her back, creeping up into her hair, his fingers tangling in the red-gold strands, gently tugging at them to tilt her head further back. Under her fingers his heart beat heavily and the warmth of his skin under that silk shirt deepened her sensual awareness of him. Her mind blurred with an explosive mixture of fear and desire and she ceased to be conscious of him at all, totally engrossed in an inner struggle with her own feelings, all her energy given over to fighting herself.

It was the first time in her life that she had ever felt like this, except on stage. The intensity of feeling of which she was capable had only had that outlet in the past. Now her whole body had become a battleground, torn by wild sensations she fought bitterly to control.

Terrified, she twisted away, wrenching back her head, a piercing cry of protest escaping from her, and Joel released her and sat back in his seat, breathing very fast, his face darkly flushed.

Suki put her shaking hands over her face, shuddering with the emotions she had just felt. She could hear the ragged intake of air as Joel breathed unsteadily beside her, but he wasn't moving or speaking and the silence between them was like a black wall.

After a time he moved at last, his hand reaching forward. The engine started again and the car purred away. He reversed in a gateway and turned the car back the way they had just come. Suki kept her face covered for a long time. Behind her fingers she was hating him, hating herself, sick with reaction. When she did drop her hands and sit up, her face averted, she knew Joel didn't look at her. He drove with his eyes straight ahead. Out of the corner of her eye she could just see the hard force of his profile. It had no expression. She didn't have a clue what he was thinking.

As they entered London again she said huskily: 'Will you drop me at Buddy's office, please?'

He gave her no answer, but ten minutes later he drew up outside the building. Suki put her hand on the door catch and felt Joel turn her way.

'Suki,' he began in a harsh, low voice, but she would not let him say whatever he had been about to say.

'Would you please open this door?' she demanded in an icy tone.

For a moment she thought he was going to refuse, force her to listen to him, then with a fierce inhalation he leant forward and said curtly: 'It's open.'

She swung the door outwards and climbed out, stumbling, her legs weak under her. She slammed the door and walked away very fast, not looking back, and heard the car streak off before she had got into the office block.

CHAPTER FOUR

'WHAT happened to you?' Buddy burst out the minute she walked into his office, his face anxious. 'I got some garbled message that you'd gone off with Joel Harlow.'

'He shanghaied me,' Suki told him, sprawling in one of the deep leather chairs beside his desk, her jean-clad legs thrust out in an attitude of weary exhaustion.

'What do you mean?'

'Picked me up outside the studio and took me for a ride,' Suki explained, while Buddy sank down on the edge of his desk, whistling under his breath, staring at her.

'Are you okay?' he asked after a pause. 'Did he try something on?'

'What do you think?' She turned her gleaming red-gold head and made a bitter face at him. 'Keep him away from me, will you? I don't ever want to see him again.'

'Right, baby,' Buddy said quickly, but he was still curious, still alarmed, his eyes fixed on her, his long thin body tensely shifting about on the desk.

'Did he . . .'

'He kissed me,' she interrupted tersely. 'That's all, but it was quite enough, thank you, and I don't want a reprise.'

Buddy relaxed slightly, grinning in wry humour. 'They will chance their luck, won't they?'

'Every time,' Suki muttered.

'You're too sexy, that's the trouble.' Buddy was beginning to laugh. 'You know, he's quite a catch, Suki. Think of all that money.' There was curiosity in his stare. 'Aren't you tempted just the slightest bit?'

'No.' She said that loudly and firmly, but inside her head there was a mocking echo. Hadn't she been? She was protesting rather too much and she knew it, but she refused to face it. Admitting anything would just make it more difficult to cope with what had happened. If she concentrated on being angry with Joel Harlow for forcing her to take those hard kisses she could channel all her explosive emotion in his direction. It was a lot easier to hate him than to hate herself, and if she ever thought about how she had felt while she was in his arms, she would start to hate herself.

Buddy sat watching her, his foot swinging. 'You know, you're pale,' he said. 'Tired. You look like someone on the verge of a breakdown. Rosie was saying only last night that you need a holiday.' He paused, shrugging. 'I guess we all do.' Turning, he leaned over the desk and picked up the big black leather schedule book, flicking over the pages with a thoughtful look in his face. 'No chance of getting away for a few weeks,' he decided aloud. 'You're booked solid right up to June. But if I keep two weeks clear in the middle of the summer we could fit in a holiday somewhere sunny and peaceful.'

Suki frowned. 'I thought I was booked solid for the whole year.'

Buddy grinned at her. 'Well, you are, baby, but I can switch the first two weeks in June until later this year.

You're supposed to be recording then and it can fit in some time in December. We can't have you folding up on us, can we? This whole outfit rides on your back.'

'Oh, that makes me feel just great,' Suki mocked, smiling at him with affection.

He put down the schedule, snapping it shut, and swung back to lean over and pat her paternally on the knee. 'We have to take care of you, don't we? At least it will shut Milly up. She's been nagging me to give you a holiday for months.'

He drove her back to the Essex house an hour later and Rosie came from the garden to look at her searchingly, her troubled expression making it clear that Buddy had told her all about what had happened. Suki gave her a brief smile and walked into the house, and Rosie followed her to her bedroom, leaning in the doorway, watching her as she sat down in front of the dressing-table mirror.

'You okay?'

'Yes.'

'I told you he was on your trail.'

'Nice to be proved right, isn't it?' In the mirror Suki's green eyes flashed towards her wryly before moving away.

'Did he bother you?' Rosie asked that quietly and Suki laughed with harsh lack of amusement.

'What a question! That depends what you mean. He certainly had every intention of bothering me, in one sense of the word, but if you're asking if he succeeded, the answer is no, he did not.' She picked up the silver-backed hairbrush and began gently brushing her hair, the loose curls tumbling around her pale face. Rosie watched her, a frown on her face.

'I suppose you know what you're doing,' she said, and Suki gave her a brief nod.

'I do,' she agreed.

'A lot of women would swoon at his feet if he so much as looked at them.'

'I've no doubt a lot already have,' Suki said cynically. 'You said yourself that he's a collector.'

Rosie nodded. 'So they say.'

'Some men collect postage stamps, some collect women,' Suki muttered. 'I've no ambition to be an entry in his catalogue.'

'You're probably wise,' Rosie said slowly.

'I'm sure I am.'

Rosie shrugged. 'Well, don't forget we're having dinner with Sir Humphrey tonight, will you? I think you should wear that white dress with the gold cord belt.'

Suki nodded and Rosie went out, closing the door behind her. As soon as she was alone Suki dropped the hairbrush with a little clatter and slowly bent her head forward into her trembling hands. She felt the blood flowing painfully in her veins, her ears singing with nervous excitement, all the aroused awareness inside her forcing itself to her attention.

Joel had been offering her a temptation which was far more powerful than he could have imagined, and there had been a few moments when she had had to fight hard to resist what he was offering her, but she knew it could only have been disastrous for her to allow herself to give in and surrender to her own feelings. It would all have been an illusion, anyway. Joel wanted her without knowing her, as other men had done before him, and he wouldn't have given her what she wanted. He would have taken her for the pleasure she could give him and left her hating herself.

She had learnt that at a very early age. Even as a very young teenager she had had spectacular looks and they had brought her a lot of sexual attention she did not want.

The children's home where she grew up had been a strictly run institution staffed by nuns who believed in a kindly but very firm discipline. The girls ate plain food, followed an unalterable routine which began early in the morning in the school chapel and was punctuated by prayer throughout the day. Life was quiet and dull and dutiful. Suki had escaped that grey emptiness as soon as she legally could. The nuns had found her a job in a local insurance office and a room of her own in a family house where the wife promised to keep an eye on her.

Unfortunately, the woman's husband soon had an eye on Suki, too, and that arrangement had only lasted a few weeks. Suki had been shaken and frightened by the way he had tried to make love to her, and she had made up her mind to leave the boring little London suburb and get a job in the centre of the city.

She managed to get a job in a London bank, found a room in a shabby lodging house, and shuttled between the two for some time in a nervous alarm towards the city life around her. Gradually she began to relax with the other girls in the office and one of them introduced her to her brother, who played the guitar. Through him, Suki met other amateur musicians and, when they realised she could sing, began going out with them to front the little group they had formed. They began to make money at it. It wasn't exactly a fortune, but if they worked a different pub each night they could make more money than any of them could by working in an office. Throughout those months before she met Buddy, Suki learnt by a series of alarming and worrying incidents to be very wary of the men she met.

She was forced to realise that she had a visual sensuality which made an immediate impact with the opposite sex. In her tight black leather jeans and low-cut shirts she looked vibrantly sexy. The green eyes held a provocative glimmer which she did not intend, which she would have suppressed if she had understood what it was that drew the men like flies towards honey. When she was singing she gave herself to the music and forgot everything else and, because she sang sexy, exciting songs, when she was performing what came through to the men listening was an impression of powerful sexuality.

Suki had begun to understand that only when Buddy, disturbed by her constant nightmares, persuaded her to see a psychiatrist. The sessions with the man had gone on for some months and had ended only when, pressed by Suki, the psychiatrist had admitted that, having uncovered the roots of her problem, he could do little else for her except advise her to come to terms with herself, her past and her present, so that she could move freely into a fully integrated future as an adjusted adult.

'There's no magic recipe,' he had told her. 'It has to be you who puts yourself together, Suki.'

'How do I do that?' she had enquired drily, and he had smiled with faintly irritating condescension at her.

'Ah, that's the question.'

'Have you got an answer?' Suki had asked, and he had shaken his head.

'The answer has to come from you.'

Suki had gone back and said to Buddy: 'I'm not paying that man to tell me questions he can't answer. What he says boils down to admitting that he doesn't know any more than I do. I'm not crazy. I have nightmares because I hated school and I would loathe to have to go back there and eat boiled cabbage and wear scratchy tunics again. There's nothing loopy about that. I'm not paying through the nose to have someone explain that to me.'

What she did not say to Buddy was that the psychiatrist had suggested to her that during her narrow, grey childhood she had been totally starved of expressed affection and that, when she was approached by men later, she had an inner struggle between her desire for the affection she had never been shown and her instinctive distrust of the motives of the men trying to make love to her.

Suki had understood and accepted what he said, but recognising the problem hadn't helped her to alter it. It didn't help her now. Joel Harlow had been one of a long line of men who had tried to coax her into bed. He was a strikingly attractive man and he had tempted her, but she didn't want what he was offering. She could have had that sort of sexual adventure any time over the past five years. She didn't want it. She wanted something far more dangerous, far more satisfying, and that he had not been offering her.

It was some time before she had recovered enough to force herself up from the dressing-table stool, her pale face taut after the fight she had had with her own emotions. She lay on the bed and made herself memorise one of the new songs Louis had just arranged for her, then she read some magazines before she took a leisurely bath. She immersed herself in sweet-scented bubbles, her tired muscles relaxing in the steamy heat of the water, listening to a radio programme and deliberately refusing to let her mind work.

Rosie banged on the door, making her jump. 'Get dressed or we'll be late for dinner!'

'Tyrant!' Suki called back, reluctantly climbing out of the bath and taking one of the huge, fluffy bath sheets from the heated towel rail on the pale yellow tiled wall.

She found the white dress draped across the bed and began to get ready. Rosie returned just as she was inspecting herself in the full-length mirrors set in the wardrobe doors. Appearing behind her in amused reflection, Rosie said: 'We're waiting for you, you know. You look fine, so come on down.'

'You told me to make an effort,' Suki retorted, still checking that she looked her best.

'So you have,' Rosie said. 'The important thing now is to be punctual. Sir Humphrey takes an old-fashioned view of people arriving late for dinner with him.'

Sir Humphrey Quine was the chairman of the huge record company which had Suki under a five-year contract. It had been signed with them two and a half years ago, when she was relatively unknown, and had seemed like a miracle to her then, but since she became a big star Buddy had been trying hard to re-negotiate the terms of it, without making much headway.

They drove into London through busy streets. Buddy was at the wheel but talked all the way, giving her a few tips on how to deal with Sir Humphrey.

'He's a devious little man, looks like Father Christmas and behaves like Fagin—watch him like a hawk.'

'We don't want you ending up as the main course at dinner,' Rosie said, and got a grin from her.

'Has he got vampire tendencies?'

'Has he?' Buddy asked rhetorically. 'He drinks a pint a day and always somebody else's, how do you think he got to be so powerful? His stock-in-trade is his kindly smile. It isn't even skin deep. Whatever he asks, the safest thing to do is hedge your bets.'

'If he asks you if you would like a glass of sherry, say you'll check with Buddy,' Rosie warned. 'On principle you don't know anything.'

Suki laughed. 'This begins to sound more like a war game than a dinner party!'

'You've got it,' said Rosie.

Suki had never actually met Sir Humphrey before— Buddy handled all that side of things and Suki normally dealt with the members of staff active on the day-to-day side of the business.

Sir Humphrey lived in a large house in Hampstead just above the Heath and looking down over the Vale of Health, the building set back behind a high brick wall and surrounded by a well-kept acre of gardens. When they were shown into the house, Suki stood looking around curiously, her fantailed mink jacket around her shoulders, the soft fur warm against her throat. A man in a dark jacket had opened the door to them and was politely removing Rosie's white fur while Buddy closely scrutinised a small oil painting hanging on the wall.

'You know what that is?' he demanded of Suki in a whisper. 'Look at that brushwork—that must have cost him a hundred thousand if it cost a penny.'

'Turn your head off,' Rosie said drily. 'It isn't done to go around working out how much people have spent on their decor.'

Buddy gave her a wounded look and stalked towards the sound of voices coming from the nearest door. Suki followed, exchanging a smile with Rosie. 'Now you've hurt his feelings.'

'Buddy hasn't got any feelings. He's made of india-rubber, he bounces when you throw him over your shoulder.'

'Have you two had a row?' Suki hated having bad feelings among those around her, it made her feel insecure.

Rosie hesitated, then shrugged and said: 'I just think he wasn't very clever over this Joel Harlow business. He practically threw you into the man's arms by inviting him to dinner, and all because big money impresses him.'

Suki stiffened, frowning. 'Can't we forget that subject? I don't want to think about Joel Harlow, let alone see him again, and I certainly don't want you and Buddy having rows over him.' She moved into the room behind Buddy, dropping her voice to a low murmur under cover of the conversation going on in the room.

Sir Humphrey bustled forward, shaking Buddy vigorously by the hand before turning to greet Suki. He was a small rotund man, his face pink and smooth and well shaven, his white hair thinning but carefully brushed forward over his head to disguise the fact, his voice and expression warmly cheerful.

'So we meet at last, Suki! I can't think why we never have before. I've been enjoying your singing for so long that it's ridiculous that we've never got around to meeting. Marvellous concert the other night; wonderful, rave reviews. Total sell-out, wasn't it? We're getting the recording out as fast as we can, believe me.'

'That's great,' Suki said with enthusiasm.

Rosie had moved closer and was oddly nudging her with her elbow and giving her funny sidelong looks which Suki could not interpret, but which, she imagined, were intended to emphasise that Buddy had described Sir Humphrey to perfection. Under the festive liveliness Suki could glimpse the tough glint of a mind like a razor, it was true.

'Rhoda, my dear, this is our star,' said Sir Humphrey, his hand under the elbow of a smiling lady of operatic dimensions who gave Suki a warm handshake and told her she had all her records. Rosie had moved even closer and was silently seething in apparent agony. While Lady Quine held forth about which of Suki's songs she liked best, Suki looked quickly at Rosie, her brows lifted in puzzled enquiry, and got a desperate roll of the eyes which made her look around the room in search of whatever had horrified Rosie so much.

She didn't have far to look. Across the room her eyes met those of the man leaning against the elegant

Adam-style fireplace. He had a glass of whisky in his hand and a totally expressionless face, and at the sight of him Suki felt her heart do a heavy somersault inside her chest.

Sir Humphrey gallantly took Suki's hand and led her around the room to meet all the other guests, some of whom she knew already. She had come prepared for an evening of possible excruciating boredom, but she had not come prepared for the sight of Joel Harlow, and she had great difficulty in keeping her smile pinned on her face.

By the time they reached Joel, he was deep in conversation with a woman whom Suki felt sure she had seen somewhere before. Sir Humphrey paused, giving Joel a fatherly look. 'Joel here tells me you and he have already met, Suki, but I gather you haven't met Angela.' He beamed. 'My niece, Angela Whitmore Angela's a textile designer, quite brilliant, her fabrics sell all over the world these days.'

'I'm quite capable of blowing my own trumpet, Uncle Humphrey,' the dark-haired woman said, smiling as she extended her hand to Suki. Slim, elegant in an ice-blue dress, she had a beautiful pale face, and her brown eyes dominated her face to the extent that they almost made you miss the delicate bone structure moulding her features.

'What sort of fabrics do you design?' Suki asked, studiously ignoring Joel's brooding stare.

'Curtain materials,' Sir Humphrey said, and got a quick, ironic look from his niece.

'Household materials of various sorts,' she expanded. 'Linens and manmade fibres.' She glanced at the curtains over the high windows behind them. 'I designed that particular fabric, actually.'

Suki looked round and was genuinely impressed by the deep blue material printed with pale pink birds and flowers in a flowing design which gave a feeling of tropical exoticism. 'That's very beautiful, you're very clever. Where do you find your inspiration?'

'For that one? From a painting by the French artist, Rousseau,' said Angela Whitmore.

'He's the chap they call the Customs Officer, isn't he?' Sir Humphrey asked blandly, and got another ironic look from his niece.

'You know he is, Uncle Humphrey.'

'Thought he was,' Sir Humphrey said with the same childlike placidity.

Angela met Suki's eyes. 'My uncle is an expert on paintings,' she said wryly. 'He's also an expert on pulling the wool over people's eyes.'

Sir Humphrey chuckled and Suki smiled at him. 'Do I thank her for the tip?'

'No man's a hero to his valet,' Sir Humphrey said, then added: 'Or, apparently, to his niece.'

'No, I wouldn't put you among my heroes, Uncle,' Angela agreed with sharp amusement.

'I don't think we'll ask her where she would put me,' he murmured to Suki, steering her away. 'Angela has a frightening tendency to say what she thinks, not my favourite method of conversation. It leads to some very awkward moments at times. I put it all down to having gone to art school—gives them bohemian ideas.' He stopped and looked at her hard. 'You didn't go to art school, did you, Suki?'

'No,' she agreed.

'Sensible girl,' he approved. 'Too much education these days, people spend years studying things and then can't get jobs.'

Suki opened her mouth to answer, but he had moved on, dragging her after him like a trophy to meet the next little cluster of guests.

'I saw you on TV last night,' a tired-looking man in a blue velvet dinner jacket murmured to her as he shook hands. 'Singing your new single, wasn't it?'

'Possibly,' Suki said, smiling back.

'Possibly?' he repeated in surprise. 'Can't you remember?'

'You probably saw a video of me,' she explained. 'I wasn't actually in the studios last night.'

'Ah,' Sir Humphrey said dreamily, 'now there's a fantastic invention, the video cassette—opens up a whole new market; enormous fortune to be made there in the future.'

Suki listened, sipping the sherry she had been given, her eye wandering away and catching Joel's cool stare. She looked quickly away. He was still with Angela Whitmore, she noted. They seemed to be on very friendly terms. Where had she seen Angela before? She couldn't pin it down at that moment, but later, as they were sitting down to dinner, it dawned on her. Angela had been the woman in flame red who had been with Joel in that nightclub the night they met. She hadn't mentioned it when Suki was introduced, but presumably she remembered it, too. Angela, for all her habit of speaking her mind, according to her uncle, could also be surprisingly discreet.

Most of the other guests were from a different milieu from the one Suki normally frequented. They talked politely and without overmuch wit about a range of subjects which she found faintly boring, from politics to money, but one thing they all had in common, they treated Joel with extreme courtesy and listened intently to every syllable he said. They all looked extremely well-to-do, but Joel Harlow was in a different league, which brought her to the next question: what was he doing here?

That was, she discovered later, a question which had also been engrossing Buddy and Rosie, as they told her after dinner when they were alone with her for a few minutes.

'I'd like to know what he's doing here,' Rosie said, and Buddy nodded.

'Didn't you say he owns N.M.A.?' Suki asked, and they both nodded at her. 'Well, maybe he and Sir Humphrey know each other through the recording business?'

'No maybe about it,' Buddy said. 'But is he here on business or pleasure?'

'Or both,' Rosie murmured drily.

'I sometimes think your minds are too suspicious,' Suki said.

'Maybe,' Buddy shrugged.

'When men like Joel Harlow and Humphrey Quine get together you can be pretty sure something's going on,' Rosie said grimly.

Suki laughed. 'I bet you look under the bed every night before you get into it!'

'You'd win your bet,' said Rosie with a wicked grin.

'I always hope there'll be a man under it.'

'Don't worry, darling, I'd protect you,' Buddy said with a wink at Suki.

'That's what I'm afraid of,' Rosie told him mournfully, just as Sir Humphrey appeared and gave Buddy a comradely beam which Buddy received with bright-eyed wariness.

'Come and tell me what you think of my vintage brandy, my dear fellow,' Sir Humphrey suggested, leading him away.

'We'd better keep tabs on them,' Rosie muttered. 'Once Buddy starts sampling vintage brandy he'll be promising Sir Humphrey that you'll sing for him for nothing.' She moved after them with a determined air and Suki was about to follow when a hand caught her elbow and she looked up with a stifled intake of air.

'Are you ignoring me, by any chance?' Joel spoke lightly, but his voice had an iron thread running through it which made her shiver.

'Oh, hello,' she said, a pulse beating at the base of her throat with such vehemence that she almost put a trembling hand up to cover the fact from his gaze.

'You looked right through me at dinner,' Joel said under his breath, and now she was certain about that hardness in his tone. She met his grey eyes directly, flinched and looked away. His powerful face held more than coldness. Unless she was very much mistaken there was a distinctly cruel line to his mouth, an angry tension which gave her the feeling she had made herself a dangerous enemy today.

CHAPTER FIVE

'I DON'T know what you're talking about,' Suki said in a faintly unsteady voice.

'Oh, yes, you do. I don't like having someone look right through me the way you've been doing all evening.'

'You're imagining things.'

'I'm imagining nothing.'

'If we haven't spoken until now it's pure accident.'

His mouth twisted savagely. 'Don't give me that, Suki. When Sir Humphrey brought you over you talked to Angela and pretended I was invisible.'

He was making her so nervous that she felt every nerve-end quivering like a plucked violin string. She glanced down, her lashes sweeping against her flushed cheek. 'Do you know Sir Humphrey well?'

'Changing the subject?' he asked curtly.

'I hadn't expected to see you here . . .' she began, and Joel interrupted with a short laugh.

'I'm sure you hadn't—or you would have had one of your headaches and ducked out of the evening, I suppose.'

'I don't have headaches,' Suki said, looking up to meet his eyes. 'I always keep professional engagements.'

The black brows shot up. 'And that's what this is?'

She half smiled. 'I'm afraid so—these people aren't

my type, you know.' She flung a glance around the room, giving a wry smile. 'No, not my type at all, any of them.'

'What is your type?'

'Musicians, singers—people in the business.' She glanced up at him, her slanting green eyes holding a smile. 'I stay in my own territory, Mr Harlow.'

'Isn't that rather limiting?' His grey eyes were hard and fierce. 'Not to say cowardly. If you refuse to risk yourself in any real relationships, Suki, you'll wither inside, you know that. Every time you refuse to take a chance you're denying that you're alive at all, and in the end you won't be, you'll be dead, a walking ghost.'

Her face was highly flushed. She threw a nervous look around, terrified someone else would have heard his low, rapid words.

'Be quiet!' she muttered, turning to fly. 'I'm not listening to you!'

She felt his hand detaining her, effortlessly wrenching her back to face him.

'Sooner or later you're going to listen, because I'm going to make sure you do,' he told her. 'You're a scared little coward, Suki.'

'I'm not!'

'God, your opinion of yourself must be rock-bottom,' he said, his eyes on her angry face.

'I don't think it's my opinion of myself that bothers you,' she retorted. 'It's my opinion of you.'

'And what's that?' His face had tautened, the strong lines of it stiff, and he watched her intently through narrowed eyes.

Suki almost backed away from giving any answer,

but something in the challenge of that stare made her lift her head in defiance and answer him.

'I think you're a man who's always had everything he wanted and has come to believe he's entitled to reach out a hand for everything he fancies,' she said.

'Charming,' he said. 'Go on.'

'Isn't that enough?'

He laughed in a low, angry way, his eyes brooding on her. 'More than enough, but I can see from your face that it isn't all you'd like to say so go ahead and say the rest.'

Suki smiled sweetly. 'Mr Harlow, I get the feeling we're playing some sort of truth game, but of a very dangerous variety.'

'Truth's always dangerous,' he said.

'Then why meddle with it?'

'In the normal way, I wouldn't,' he said. 'I'd realise you didn't like me and walk away without a backward glance.'

'Then why don't you do just that?' she demanded hurriedly, getting a direct, hard stare from those grey eyes.

'Because I want you too badly to do anything of the kind.'

She caught back a startled gasp, lowering her eyes, and felt him take a step closer. Softly he went on: 'And because the more I see of you the more I realise you've been in a deep-freeze for years, and you're so packed in ice you don't even realise it. But I've seen you singing and I know that isn't all there is to you—under the ice there's more passion than you know what to do with—and I want it, Suki. I want to be the one to smash through the ice and unleash all that burning feeling.'

Suki trembled, glancing around in scarlet embarrassment to make sure nobody else was in earshot. She caught Angela Whitmore's watchful eyes and hurriedly looked back at Joel.

'Be quiet!' she whispered. 'What do you think you're doing, talking to me like that with all these people around?'

'If you don't like it, give me a chance to talk to you alone,' he came back at once.

'No!' she burst out.

'I'm not going away, Suki, and I'm not giving up.'

Her eyes flickered over his face, reading the fixed, immovable determination with a sinking sense of shock and dismay. His eyes were steady and implacable, glinting in silvery appraisal as she met them, his taut cheekbones leading the eye down to that strong jawline. She searched that face for some sign of uncertainty and found none. He meant what he said. She had been pursued many times in the past, but they had always given up when she made it clear that she didn't want to know. Joel Harlow was made of different stuff. He wasn't giving up.

'You'll be wasting your time,' she said at last with husky unsteadiness.

'I don't think so,' he told her. 'I might have done if you hadn't encouraged me.'

'I did nothing of the kind!'

'Oh, yes,' he mocked. 'When I kissed you . . .'

Colour swept up her face to her hairline and she half turned away to hide it from him. Softly he added: 'It confirmed my suspicions. The passion's in there, all right, and all it needs is the right man to break through to it.'

'That won't be you,' Suki muttered.

'Oh, yes, it will. I don't care how long it takes, you see, or what I have to do to get you, but the minute you came on stage that night I knew I had to have you. You set the whole place on fire. I couldn't take my eyes off you.' He smiled drily. 'You may deny it, but what you sell is dreams, and you certainly sold one to me that night. I won't be satisfied until I find that beautiful, sexy body of yours in my bed and know you belong to me.'

She had listened in rigid attention, her eyes on the floor, and as he stopped talking she looked up slowly. 'Thanks for the warning,' she said in a voice harsh with anger.

'If you had any honesty at all, you'd face the fact that you aren't happy with yourself the way you are,' Joel told her. 'How can you be? You aren't alive at all, you only live when you're on that stage singing, and that's because only then can you dare to release any of that passion inside you.'

'It never crosses your mind that all your guesswork about me could be way off beam, I suppose?' Suki asked coldly.

'No,' said Joel, amusement flashing across his face.

'You've got a vivid imagination, Mr Harlow,' she snapped, and got a mocking glance.

'Oh, very vivid,' he agreed, and the look in those derisive grey eyes made her look hurriedly away.

'Just stay away from me,' she told him, and his

amusement seemed to deepen.

'There's a ring of desperation in the way you said that.'

'I'm glad you noticed, I was beginning to wonder what I would have to say to get the message home to you.' She forced herself to meet his eyes again, her spine rigid. 'Mr Harlow, let me put it very simply. I'm not interested in having an affair with you. I don't jump into bed with anyone and I'm not making an exception for you. There are plenty of willing ladies, I should think, why harass me? Why can't you just leave me alone and accept the fact that I don't want you?' She turned away on the last low, angry words and walked towards Buddy and Rosie before he could stop her. They were with Sir Humphrey on the other side of the room and Buddy was very flushed.

Rosie gave Suki a smile as she joined them. 'Having a good time?' She was flushed, too. The vintage brandy must be very good, thought Suki. Rosie wasn't anywhere near being tipsy, but she was definitely enjoying herself.

Sir Humphrey tried to persuade Suki to try some, but she politely refused.

'Suki doesn't drink much at all,' Buddy explained.

'Good girl,' said Sir Humphrey, pouring himself another glass of the amber liquid and tilting it to his lips with a satisfied smile.

Rosie looked at Suki thoughtfully. 'Tired?'

She nodded, smiling.

'I'm afraid we shall have to leave, Sir Humphrey,' said Rosie, turning back to their host. 'Suki needs a good night's rest.'

'Tired?' Sir Humphrey focused on her vaguely, his face very pink. 'You look washed out. You're working her too hard, my dear fellow. All work and no play, remember.'

'She's going to have a holiday, soon,' Buddy assured him. 'In a few weeks.'

'News to me,' Rosie said. 'When was this decided?'

'Take her somewhere peaceful,' said Sir Humphrey, patting her bare arm with a fatherly hand. 'That's what she needs—a few weeks in the sun doing nothing at all.'

'It sounds fantastic,' Suki agreed, smiling.

'I've got a villa in the Bahamas, that's where Rhoda and I go to escape from it all.' He looked at Buddy with a cheerful smile. 'If you want somewhere really private why don't you use my place? It has a private beach, you wouldn't get any trouble from the local people. No fans or autograph-hunters there.' He clapped Buddy on the shoulder vigorously. 'I'll be in touch, dear fellow, I'll be in touch.'

In the car as they drove back through the silent dark streets of the city, Buddy said discontentedly: 'I didn't get any promises out of the old vulture, you notice. Ask him for better terms for Suki and what does he do— offers to lend us his villa in the Bahamas for a fortnight.'

'It was a dinner party, after all,' Suki said. 'What did you expect?'

'I hoped to get him to admit that that contract's no longer valid,' Buddy growled.

'Optimist! I told you that you'd be wasting your time with him. A contract's a contract and he knows you can't wriggle out of it.' Rosie had kicked off her shoes and was massaging her small, thin feet with a blissful expression. 'I'm so tired I could just die!'

Suki stared out of the window at the yellow street lamps flashing past, and drew her jacket closer around her, the softness of the fur comforting against her cheek.

'You got cornered by Joel Harlow again, I noticed,' Rosie said beside her, and she looked round.

'I couldn't get away.'

'No wonder he's stinking rich—he doesn't give up, does he?'

'No,' said Suki, shivering.

Rosie was watching her. 'Sir Humphrey gave the game away—he told us Joel Harlow asked to be invited tonight. Apparently Sir Humphrey casually mentioned the fact that you'd be there and Joel at once said he would like to come.'

'There's something scary about that guy,' Buddy said. 'Whatever you do he just keeps on coming. I wouldn't like to face him across a negotiating table.' He chuckled under his breath. 'Sir Humphrey's bad enough, heaven knows. Harlow would be ten times worse. What a poker player—that face doesn't give a thing away. I had a little chat with him tonight, trying to find out if there was anything cooking between him and Sir Humphrey, and I didn't get a flicker out of him.'

'Well, maybe there isn't,' said Suki.

'Maybe,' Rosie said in a doubtful tone.

'What a wasted evening!' Buddy sighed. He drove in silence for a while, then said: 'Damned if I don't take

Sir Humphrey up on that offer of the villa. You can bet he doesn't expect me to—but I will, just to annoy him.'

'You can be so adult,' Rosie murmured, smiling. 'Why don't you go and kick his windows in as well?'

'Don't tempt me, I might just do it,' said Buddy.

'No wonder people say women are the better half,' Rosie said to nobody in particular.

'Who says? Women, I suppose.' Buddy was travelling at speed along the flat, winding Essex lanes towards their house, most of his attention on the dark road ahead. Suki lay back, eyes closed, hearing their light voices washing over her without listening to any more of what they said. She felt grey and on the verge of tears, although she couldn't think why she should. Joel Harlow had managed to depress her. His persistence troubled her and she wished she could think of a way of getting it home to him that he was just wasting his time.

She was somehow half afraid that everywhere she went from now on Joel Harlow would turn up, but over the following week she saw nothing of him at all and was able to work without interruption. For some strange reason she was no longer finding work as totally engrossing as she had done over the past five years. She threw herself into it with grim determination, but her singing lacked some of its usual sparkle, and Buddy commented with a frown on that.

'You really do need a holiday, kid. We're going to have to do something about that.'

Suki grinned at him teasingly. 'I thought you were going to make Sir Humphrey keep his word about that villa in the Bahamas?'

'When I get around to it,' Buddy said. 'That'll teach him.'

Rosie was looking unlike herself, too, Suki thought the next morning as Rosie went through her wardrobe to find the right outfit for another photo-call planned for later that day. A magazine was coming to the house to do a photo-spread on Suki, and Rosie always chose what she should wear on these occasions.

'You're pale,' Suki said.

Rosie didn't look round, but Suki distinctly saw her stiffen.

'Got a cold?' Suki asked, because Rosie was one of those people who got colds badly and, when one degree under, could be white and drawn. That was how she looked today, Suki thought, as Rosie turned towards her with several outfits over her arm.

'I'm fine,' Rosie said, not meeting her eyes, and Suki watched her with even more concern. Rosie was lying, that was obvious, and Suki found that very worrying, because it was not like Rosie to be secretive about anything. Rosie went out and for a few minutes Suki sat there, frowning, looking back over the last few days and realising that Rosie had been rather muted for some time.

She tackled Buddy on the subject later that day and he looked at her blankly.

'Wrong with Rosie? I hadn't noticed anything wrong with her. What are you talking about? She had a bit of a headache this morning, that's all.'

Suki met his eyes and saw that Buddy genuinely had not noticed anything, so she dropped the subject. That evening Rosie was quite lively and talkative and Buddy came in for some of her usual teasing, but Suki noticed that once or twice Rosie lapsed into an odd, tired blankness from which she visibly roused herself with an effort the minute Buddy looked at her.

There *was* something wrong, and either it was physical or had a physical effect, because the following morning when she saw Rosie walking in the garden doing some pruning among the roses, Suki thought she looked even whiter, her face set in weary lines.

Suki dressed in jeans and a green shirt and went out into the spring sunshine to join her. Rosie looked round, forcing a quick smile.

'Hi.'

'Busy?' Suki asked. There was a wicker trug on the grass, and Rosie was dropping rose clippings into it neatly.

'I like to get in some gardening now and then,' Rosie said. 'It takes your mind off things.'

'What things?' Suki watched her as she asked that and saw Rosie's eyes flicker nervously.

'Oh, business,' Rosie said, and Suki leaned over to breathe in the scent of some hyacinths in a long stone trough, the dark blue of their tiny flowers so vivid it took your breath away. She pretended to be engrossed in them while she was secretly watching Rosie, her anxiety growing.

'Why won't you tell me, Rosie?' she asked at last, swinging round to face her and Rosie visibly jumped.

'What?' She pretended to laugh, but her pale mouth quivered. Rosie was a slight, elegant woman who had kept her youthful figure although she was now in her fortieth year. Her hair had once been blonde, but she had had it tinted a silvery colour to hide the increasing streaks of grey invading it. When she was in good health she had a lively, mobile face full of sparkling energy, but her colouring meant that when she was not at her best she could seem washed out and grey.

'Something is wrong—I know it is. Is it to do with the business?'

Rosie laughed in an oddly grim way. 'No.'

'Then what? Are you ill? Is something wrong with you?'

Rosie stared at her, hesitating.

'Tell me,' Suki pleaded. 'You're worrying me.'

Rosie made a wry face. 'Then that makes two of us. I didn't want to worry you. I'd have got round to it sooner or later, but I needed time. I haven't got over the shock yet, myself.'

'What shock?'

Rosie slowly took off her gardening gloves and dropped them into the trug. Turning, she walked away across the grass towards the low stone wall which ran around the coloured paving stones of the patio beside the house, and Suki followed her. Rosie perched on the top of the wall, gripping it with both hands, her eyes fixed on the blue spring sky above them. The trees were coming into full leaf, a pale green haze cloaking the outline of the elms on the distant horizon where the fields ran into the sky.

'I'm pregnant,' Rosie said abruptly, and Suki's mouth dropped open in astonishment and disbelief.

'*What?*'

'Pregnant,' Rosie repeated, and then laughed grimly. 'But I can't blame you for the sheer incredulity. I felt the same myself. I couldn't believe it, either.'

'Rosie!' Suki burst out, staring at her in wide-eyed excitement. 'You're not pulling my leg?'

'My sense of humour wouldn't stretch that far,' Rosie said. 'I'd be as likely to make jokes about having bubonic plague.'

'But aren't you glad?' Suki was recovering from her first shock now and feeling as though Rosie had just told her fantastic news, but she could see Rosie didn't feel very happy about it at all. 'Don't you want the baby? I thought you couldn't have any. I didn't ask because I didn't want to upset you.'

Dark coins of colour crept into Rosie's cheeks. 'It isn't me, it's Buddy,' she said.

'I'd have thought Buddy loved children!'

'Not to the extent of having any of his own,' Rosie said. 'He was frank about that when we got married. No kids, he said. They disrupt your life.'

'But you,' Suki said gently. 'Don't you want a baby, Rosie?'

'Me?' Rosie looked down, sighing. 'Suki, I'm forty years old, I'm past it.'

'If you were, you wouldn't be pregnant,' Suki said teasingly, and saw her laugh with reluctance.

'You know what I mean. Think of all the nuisance— nappies and tins of baby food and that awful howling they make, like banshees in the middle of the night. I'd have to stop working with Buddy, stay at home pretending to be domesticated, which I'm not and never have been. I can't see myself as the motherly type.'

'I can,' said Suki. 'You'd make a wonderful mother and if you can't face the nappy-changing, etc., why not get a nanny? You and Buddy have the money.'

'Don't be so logical,' Rosie pleaded. 'I'm feeling too fragile for that today.'

'You haven't told Buddy, I take it?'

'I can't face the idea. I can just imagine how he's going to react.'

Suki paused, a dart of uncertainty shooting through her. 'It is Buddy's . . .' She broke off, flushing, and Rosie gave her a wry look.

'Yes, it is, so you can wipe that look off your face. I've never looked at another man in fifteen years of marriage.' She halted, her eyes faintly amused. 'Well,' she conceded, 'I might look now and then—who doesn't? Something like Joel Harlow would make any red-blooded woman look twice. But it doesn't mean a thing, just an occasional brush with fantasy. Buddy suits me. We suit each other. That's partly what's worrying me.'

'Why does that worry you?'

'For fifteen years there's just been the two of us— what's it going to do to our marriage to have a third one around all the time?'

Suki considered this thoughtfully. 'You've had me around for the last five years and it hasn't done any harm to your marriage.'

'That's different,' Rosie said frankly. 'You haven't disrupted anything. You're really very easy to deal with, Suki, and anyway, if it hadn't worked out to have you around it would have been a simple matter to find you somewhere else to live. You aren't able to be that elastic with a kid of your own. You've got it and you're stuck with it for the duration.'

'I think Buddy will be thrilled,' Suki told her.

'I wish I had your childlike faith!'

'Don't most men fancy the idea of being a father?'

'Buddy isn't most men, any more than I'm most women. We've had a great scene going between us for fifteen years and now it's going to get clobbered.'

Suki walked along the wall, running her hand over the cold stone and frowning. She found Rosie's reaction to the fact of her pregnancy disturbing and upsetting. A blackbird began to sing on the gable of the roof, his orange beak a splash of vibrant colour against the blue sky. Suki watched him with blank eyes. She felt strangely cold, although the sun was quite warm out of the wind.

'Haven't you thought about the baby?' she asked with her back to Rosie. 'It's coming, whether you want it or not, and it's going to need your love.'

Rosie was silent and when she turned Suki saw her frowning. 'I'd forgotten,' Rosie said slowly. 'Hey, I'm stupid, aren't I? I should have remembered how you'd feel, Suki. Don't look so shattered. Have I destroyed your illusions?'

'I haven't got any,' Suki said. 'Never mind me, anyway. It's the baby that matters. Buddy's a grown man . . .'

'Do you want a bet? He may look pretty grown up from the outside, but remember what he's like when he doesn't get his own way? He reverts at top speed to the age of six.'

'All the same, he could get by without having his own way, but a baby's so helpless, Rosie. You've *got* to love it!' Suki tried to stop the raw sound entering her voice, but Rosie caught it and looked at her intently.

'Suki, I'm not going to dump the baby,' she said with an attempt at humour which didn't quite come off. 'Oh, I'm just having a moan, take no notice—this baby will have the best of everything, you know that.'

'All it really needs is love,' Suki said earnestly.

Rosie nodded. She got up from the wall, shivering. 'That wind is turning nasty, let's go in, shall we?' As they walked back to the house Rosie asked: 'Have you ever thought of trying to find your mother, Suki?'

'No, I haven't,' Suki answered with a bitter force that hurt in the back of her throat. 'I wouldn't want to know her, to know anything about her. I know all I need to know. She left me to die—what else do I need to know? How could anybody do a thing like that?'

'Maybe it wasn't her,' said Rosie. 'Maybe somebody else did it. I mean, after all, when a woman's just had a baby isn't the time she'd choose to go walking around the streets, is it?'

'But she had to know about it,' said Suki. 'She had to agree, otherwise she would have come forward when it was in the papers. It made the front page, they told me.' She laughed angrily. 'I was news from the day I was born—but don't ever tell anyone so, will you?'

Rosie said quickly: 'Of course not,' then with a sigh said: 'You know, it would make a fantastic piece of publicity. What a story!'

Suki bristled. 'I'd never forgive anyone who spilled it to the press!'

'I know,' Rosie said hastily. 'And we wouldn't, you know we never have.'

'No—thanks.' Suki muttered the words harshly.

'But I think if I'd been you I would have been very tempted to find out what was behind it,' Rosie went on.

'It's obvious what was behind it. She didn't want me.'

'There could be a dozen different reasons, Suki. She must have been pretty desperate to do a thing like that.'

'I don't care how desperate she was!'

'Aren't you curious, though? It might make you feel easier about it all if you knew why.'

Suki stopped dead, turning a white face to her. 'Don't ask me to sympathise with someone who tried to kill me when I was barely a few hours old, Rosie, because you'd have your work cut out. The only feeling I have for my mother, whoever she was, is contempt. No reason in the world could be strong enough to excuse her.'

Rosie looked as though she was going to argue, then she sighed. 'I understand how you feel.'

'Do you?' Suki stared at her. 'Then don't talk about your baby as though it was nothing but a nuisance, Rosie. It isn't like you, and it hurts to hear you talk like that.'

'You ever been sick every morning for a week?' Rosie enquired drily. 'I'll have to tell Buddy soon, because as sure as God made little green apples it's sooner or later going to occur to him that there's something funny going on if I keep rushing into the bathroom with my hand over my mouth every morning.'

Suki was forced into uneven laughter. 'Oh, poor Rosie, I'm sorry—is it really that bad?'

'It's no picnic.' Rosie opened the door. 'I'm forty, for heaven's sake. It isn't going to be fun for me.'

'Have you seen a doctor?'

Suki had forgotten how her voice carried and when Buddy appeared in the door of his office, looking worried, she could have kicked herself.

'Seen a doctor? What's wrong now?' he growled.

'Can you get a megaphone?' Rosie demanded of Suki sarcastically. 'Sure you wouldn't like to broadcast to the whole neighbourhood?'

'What's going on around here? I'm trying to work, keep it down!' Buddy snapped, banging back into his study, then popping out again to ask: 'Why do you need to see a doctor, anyway?' He peered at her. 'You do look like a ship's biscuit, now I come to think of it. Some female trouble again, I suppose?'

'So concerned and thoughtful, isn't he?' Rosie demanded of nobody in particular, her face flushed.

'Don't tell me if you don't want to,' shrugged Buddy. 'I don't know anything about a woman's internal workings, anyway.'

'Well, maybe I'll draw you a diagram,' Rosie said, pushing him back into his office and following. The door shut and a moment later Suki jumped as Buddy gave a squawk of indeterminate sound. Rosie had, she gathered, told him.

CHAPTER SIX

WHEN she saw Buddy that afternoon, he looked like a man in a state of extreme shock, his flyaway hair ruffled wildly, as though he had spent most of the day tearing it with his hands. He looked at her bolt-eyed as he flung himself into a chair in the lounge, his long thin legs moving with his usual disjointed yet graceful energy.

'I can't get over it!'

'Aren't you thrilled?' Suki asked. 'Isn't it exciting?'

'Exciting? Suki, I don't even believe it's true yet. Every five minutes I think: Rosie's going to have a baby, and every time I get dizzy. Out of the blue like that, after fifteen years, it isn't easy to believe.'

'I think it's wonderful,' Suki said.

'Life's never going to be the same again,' Buddy groaned.

'Think how much fun you'll have!'

'Look, I know what happens when there's a baby in a house—I've seen it happen before. The house is turned upside down. Everything revolves around the damned baby, nothing else matters any more.'

Suki laughed, wondering if Buddy was suffering pangs of jealousy over the coming baby, but unable to believe such a ridiculous idea. Or was it ridiculous? He had had Rosie's undivided attention for fifteen years, but a baby would nudge him out of the lime-light.

He put his fingers over his face, wailing behind them. 'And what's everyone going to say? At our age? We're going to look like idiots!'

'I'd guess all the men will think you're quite a guy,' Suki said cheerfully. 'Becoming a father at forty-four . . .'

'Five,' Buddy said.

'Even more impressive.'

She felt him peering at her through his fingers. 'I guess it isn't bad,' he admitted.

'They'll all envy you. Having a baby in the house will make you feel years younger, I'd think.'

'Starting a family at our age? You're crazy!'

'I think it's wonderful.' She smiled at him. 'Put me on the rota for baby-sitting, won't you? I see myself as a sort of auntie.'

For a few minutes Buddy was silent, then he said: 'I keep trying to think of a way of leading up to the subject with my friends.'

'Buy a box of the best Havanas and hand them out,' Suki said. 'Don't apologise, Buddy—boast!'

He grinned, dropping his hands. 'Now there you might have something.' His eyes took on a visionary look. 'It'll certainly cause something of a sensation. Just picture their faces!'

'It will improve your image no end,' Suki mocked. 'Nothing like potential fatherhood to give you a virile image.'

Buddy wasn't listening. 'I wonder what it'll be,' he said to himself. 'I might not mind so much if it was a boy.'

'Well, of all the sexist remarks!'

'I'm no chauvinist,' Buddy denied. 'But I must say I wouldn't mind having a son to take on the business when I've retired. I haven't done too badly and there'd be quite a nice little agency for him to inherit one day.'

'Empire-builder!' Suki mocked.

He laughed. 'I suppose I'll get used to the jokes,' he added, and she smiled at him.

'Of course you will. The best defence is always attack, anyway, you told me that yourself years ago when I did my first press interviews. Don't give them a chance to make the jokes—make them yourself.'

'Oh, I will,' Buddy agreed. He sobered. 'How do you think Rosie is going to stand up to this, though? I hope she isn't going to have a bad time with this baby. She isn't young any more.'

'Forty? That isn't the onset of senility, you know,' Suki argued. 'Lots of women have babies at forty.'

'Do they?' Buddy looked doubtful. 'My sister had all hers while she was in her twenties.' He grinned. 'I remember how she queened it over Rosie when she had the last one. It made Rosie so mad I could almost see the smoke coming out of her ears! Women can be so patronising to each other. If Megan tries it on with Rosie now she'll get a punch in the nose.' He got up suddenly. 'You know what? I'm going to ring Megan now and tell her.'

'Ask Rosie.' Suki said, but she said it to an empty room. Buddy had hurried out and hadn't heard a word.

'I don't believe it,' Rosie complained the next day. 'He's been on the phone almost non-stop for hours. I'm surprised he doesn't ring the White House and tell them.'

Suki laughed. 'I think he's getting rather pleased with himself. He was up very early this morning, wasn't he?'

'And bouncing about like a kangaroo,' Rosie agreed. She was just as pale this morning, dark shadows under her eyes. 'He never even noticed I was sick again.'

'Have you seen the doctor about this morning sickness? Can't they stop it?'

Rosie grimaced. 'Oh, I saw him, how do you think I knew? Do you know what I thought was wrong? I had a horrible feeling I'd got some fatal illness—it never entered my head that I was pregnant. When I finally plucked up the nerve to go and see the doctor he did some tests and when he told me he was grinning like a fool. I wouldn't believe him at first. When I told him about the morning sickness he said stay in bed and eat a couple of dry biscuits before you get up.'

'And it doesn't work?'

'Not so far. I hate dry biscuits, too.'

'Poor Rosie,' said Suki with amusement.

'I don't see anything funny about it,' protested Rosie. 'I think I could have stood it better if Buddy had been as appalled as I'd expected, but after his first horrified screams he started enjoying himself, and that makes me so mad I could spit!'

'I thought you were mainly worried about his reaction. Aren't you relieved he's beginning to be pleased?'

Rosie looked at her in a faintly sulky way. 'I suppose so, but I can't help resenting the fact that he seems to think all the credit goes to him. Haven't you ever noticed how infuriating it is when you're feeling grim to have someone about who keeps seeing everything through rose-tinted spectacles?'

'You need a holiday,' Suki told her.

'Then that makes two of us.' Rosie glanced at the door of Buddy's office. 'I'll tackle him about that when he finally gets off the phone. Anyone would think it was him having this baby!'

Suki laughed, looking at her watch. 'I'll have to rush, I've got an appointment with Louis at eleven. I'm not happy with those new arrangements.'

'Too fast for you, aren't they?'

'Much too fast. Louis says not, but then he doesn't have to sing them. My tongue gets twisted with some of those lines.'

She drove into London in her Ferrari and parked it in an underground car park near Louis's office. He was in a dogmatic mood and it took her some time to persuade him she couldn't sing the new songs the way he wanted them sung.

At last he caved in, rather sullenly, and she got up to go. 'Lunch?' Louis suggested, looking at his watch.

Suki hesitated briefly, then smiled at him. 'Thanks, I'd love to.'

They went round the corner to a small Chinese restaurant which did, Louis assured her, the best Chinese cooking in London. He was well known there and was greeted with warmth by the owner. They at once went into a cosy huddle over the menu, discussing at length which meals were particularly good that day.

Suki glanced around the crowded room and caught a smile. She looked again and then smiled back, recognising the young man with the fluffy dark blond hair, the colour of liquid honey, his round blue eyes deceptively frank and childlike. He got up and wandered over.

'Snap,' he said, kissing her.

'Hallo, Richie, what are you doing in England? I thought you were living in the States these days.'

'Yeah, I'm over here for a few days to do some recording. I see you had a big concert the other day. Went down big, did it?'

She nodded. 'Sell-out.'

'Crazy!' He shook hands with Louis and sat down at the table. 'I can't stop, I'm with my agent and the minute I'm out of his sight he might sell me to someone. How are you, Louis? How's Buddy?' Richie had once been in Buddy's stable, but after he went to America he had cut his connection with the agency and Suki hadn't seen him for several years.

'Rosie's having a baby,' Louis told him, and Richie whistled in laughing disbelief.

'No kidding?'

'Straight up,' Louis said, and Richie sat shaking his head and laughing over the idea of Buddy as a father at forty-five.

'Who'd have thought it?' It must have knocked them over. Are they happy about it?'

'Buddy's over the moon,' Louis said, but he looked at Suki with wry curiosity. 'How *does* Rosie feel, by the way? You know, I just don't see her as the motherly type. She and Buddy have never struck me as needing anybody else, know what I mean? I mean, some people you know they're family types, but Buddy and Rosie? No.'

'She's getting used to the idea,' Suki said, crossing her fingers under the table.

'Your new L.P. is great,' Louis told Richie. 'Especially your own songs—nobody sings them like you, nobody. How's it going in the States?'

'Like hot cakes,' Richie said modestly, tossing back that soft blond hair in a satisfied movement and smiling to himself. He looked up. 'Hey, is the whisper true? Is Harlow buying into Style?'

Suki sat up, the smile whisked away from her face. 'Where did you hear that?'

'My agent,' Richie said. 'He knows everything. You're with Style, aren't you, Suki? Have you heard anything?'

Louis and Suki looked at each other.

'No,' Suki said. 'But Joel Harlow was at a dinner party Sir Humphrey gave the other night. Buddy wondered what he was doing there.'

'According to my agent, Harlow has bought Sir Humphrey's interest in Style and is trying to buy up enough from other people to give him a controlling interest.'

'There's bound to be opposition to that,' Louis murmured, frowning. 'Nobody's going to like the idea. Somebody's sure to get the government to interfere. What does Harlow want a British record company for, anyway?'

'The more they've got, the more they want,' Richie told him cynically.

'True,' Louis agreed.

Richie got up, looking over his shoulder at the table where his agent sat impatiently staring at them. 'I must get back before he eats the knives and forks. Lovely to see you, Suki. When the L.P. of your concert comes out, I'll rush off to buy it.' He bent and kissed her lightly, waved a hand at Louis and walked away.

'Nice boy,' Louis said.

'Very.' Suki had forgotten Richie already. She was far too busy turning over what he had told them about Joel's machinations with Style, wondering if it was true that Sir Humphrey had sold him his shares in the firm and, if it was true, just what Joel was up to and what he planned to do. She spent most of the time she was with Louis thinking along the same lines, hardly noticing what she ate, and Louis couldn't help observing her total abstraction.

'Next time we have lunch I'll bring a book,' he said as they parted, and she grinned apologetically at him.

'Sorry, my mind was on other things. I wasn't good company today, I'm afraid.'

Louis gave her a shrewd stare. 'Worrying about Joel Harlow and what's going on at Style? I shouldn't let it bother your pretty little head, sweetheart. It won't affect you. You're far too important to them for it to make an atom of difference to you.'

Suki smiled politely, but as she turned away her expression was wry. It wouldn't make any difference to her, would it? He had no idea. She had intended to pick up her car and drive back to Essex when she left Louis, but her mind was too blown by Richie's bombshell about Joel. She had to be alone. She wandered away into the spring sunshine without any idea where she was going. She hadn't had any free time for years and wasn't quite sure what to do with herself. Wearing dark glasses and a headscarf tied over her betraying red-gold hair, she was able to walk along Bond Street among the hurrying crowds without any danger of being recognised. It was a long time since she had window-shopped alone, following her own impulse if she saw something she liked, and it was rather fun.

Emerging outside the gates of St James's Park she made her way along the path under the trees, walking slowly, her hands in her pockets, her sheepskin coat swinging loosely around her slender hips, her mind drifting back of its own accord to Joel Harlow. She had told herself over and over again to stop thinking about him, but the moment she took her guard off it, her stupid mind returned to the subject which had been obsessing her ever since lunch.

That was worrying in itself. In the past, she had dismissed every man who tried to get close to her without even thinking twice about it, but Joel Harlow refused to be dismissed, either from her life or from her mind, apparently. From the minute she saw him she had had this uneasy, disturbed sensation about him, recognising an implicit threat to herself in him. Or was the threat inside her, rather than directed against her by Joel? She had had her feelings in cold storage for so long she couldn't quite be certain what it was she felt towards him.

The burning intensity of emotion of which she was capable frightened her, except when she was channelling it safely into her music, and although she tried to deny it to herself she couldn't be unaware of the fact

that somehow Joel had the capacity to put down a
taproot to that stored feeling. He threatened her,
threatened the safe refuge in which she sheltered,
his presence capable of tearing it down around her and
exposing her to elements within herself she dreaded. It
is only if your ability to feel is potentially explosive that
you need to guard against emotion, and Suki flinched
away from anyone or anything which might unleash
her tethered feelings.

It was a pity, she thought grimly, that Joel had seen
her sing that night. She knew she had been giving out
with everything she had, her whole being flowing over
the footlights. If they had first met next day he would
have seen her cool and withdrawn and guarded. First
impressions can be dangerous.

What was he doing, buying into Style? She paused,
shivering, her eyes fixed on the green distance of the
park, the black shadows of the trees wavering on the
asphalt path as the wind moved their branches. Was
it purely coincidence? Or was it a deliberate eruption
into her life? She stood there, frowning, her hands
deep in her pockets. It was ridiculous to suspect that
any man, however rich, would buy his way into a huge
record company merely to force his way into her life,
she told herself. Nobody would be so crazy.

All the same, she couldn't help remembering the
glittering insistence of Joel's eyes at Sir Humphrey's
party, the low fierce voice with which he had warned
her that he meant to have her. Something in the stark
bone structure of his face, a hint of primitive force
and obsessed will, had made what he said to her
deeply disturbing. Joel Harlow was a man who had

always got what he wanted and saw no reason why anyone should be allowed to refuse him. Men who have never failed to achieve their goal become fanatic about getting their own way, their ego unable to take a denial because that would disturb their idea of themselves.

She had walked right through the park and come out the other side. She wasn't conscious of feeling tired, her mind too hyper-active for her body, and when it came on suddenly to rain she was surprised, shaken out of her thoughts when a raindrop hit her cheek. The rain intensified, soaking her scarf to her head and blinding her. She ran towards a nearby office doorway, halting under the silvery metal canopy above the swing doors. Huddled in her coat, she turned to peer out into the sheets of rain just as a long black limousine drew up at the kerb.

Absently, Suki watched the chauffeur get out, open an umbrella and walk round to open the door for his passenger, holding the umbrella above him as he slid out. Suki's eyes widened in horrified shock as she saw that it was Joel.

She swung the other way, freezing on the spot, not even daring to run in case that drew his attention to her. In her saturated coat and headscarf and with her back to him it was more than likely that he wouldn't recognise her, wouldn't even notice her as he walked past into the building.

She heard the car door slam, heard the ring of footsteps on the wet pavement, her attention intently focused on them. When they went on past her she felt herself begin to tremble with relief and was about to rush away when she heard them stop dead. She tensed just as Joel strode across the space between them and seized her arm, swinging her round.

She looked up nervously into his face as he demanded: 'What the hell are you doing there?'

Before she could answer that she was running his eye down over her and frowning. 'You're saturated, you look like a drowned cat!' His fingers tightened round her arm, pushing her towards the door into the office block.

'Let go!' Suki protested, struggling against that controlling hand. 'What do you think you're doing?' She paused, searching for some excuse to give for being there, and added: 'I'm waiting for someone.'

He looked at her with grim incredulity. 'Out there? In the rain? Who for?'

She hadn't thought that far when she lied to him and there was a split second pause before she came up with a name, and it was the name she had had on her mind all the time as she walked in the park. 'Richie Derby.'

Joel's eyes narrowed. He slowly lifted his head and glanced up and down the street, his mouth twisting. 'He doesn't seem to be coming,' he said derisively, looking back at her. 'And from the look of you, you've been waiting a long time. Stood you up, did he?' She felt a rush of angry colour fill her face at the mocking question and snapped back.

'Obviously he's been delayed.'

'Obviously,' Joel mocked, then made an impatient face. 'You can come up and dry in my office,' he informed her, turning to stride away across the foyer of the building with Suki scurrying after him helplessly, tethered to him by one wrist.

'Look,' she panted, Richie will wonder where I am . . .'

'Shut up,' said Joel, pushing her into a lift. The doors slid to and the lift rose silently. Suki leaned on the wall, biting her lip, her eyes on the floor, aware that Joel was staring fixedly at her. He leaned over and she jumped about six feet in the air, her gaze flying to his face. He gave her a dry glance and whipped the wet scarf off her head.

The lift stopped and the doors softly parted. Joel stepped out, grabbing Suki's wrist again, and with alarmed surprise she saw that a deputation was waiting for them, a row of men in dark suits and flatteringly welcoming smiles.

Joel nodded to them and said curtly: 'I'll be with you in a quarter of an hour, would you wait in the boardroom, please?' He didn't wait for an answer from them, merely turned and walked away, taking Suki with him, while the men stared after them in silence. What on earth must they be thinking, she thought, and would any of them have recognised her?

Joel pushed open a door and Suki found herself being thrust into a beautifully furnished room which she imagined must be a private suite attached to the boardroom. Joel released her and walked away across the smooth ivory-coloured carpet. 'Take off your coat,' he said over his shoulder. 'You're dripping on the carpet.'

She bristled. 'Will you stop ordering me around?'

He had opened a tall cabinet on the far side of the room and was taking out two glasses. 'You need a drink,' he said casually, ignoring her own protest. 'Stop standing over there. You're not leaving.'

'Who says I'm not?'

'I do.' He poured whisky into both glasses and she stared at the long, smooth line of his back in the elegant dark lounge suit, hating him. The moment she was in his company she felt this electric awareness of him which scared the life out of her and she was bitterly afraid he knew what effect he could have on her.

He swung to face her in a lithe movement. 'Get that wet coat off and come and sit down,' he ordered in a tone which made the hair on the back of her neck prickle aggressively.

She would have argued if some expression in the depths of those hard grey eyes hadn't warned her that if she did she might not enjoy the consequences. After a pause she moved her hand upward and with trembling fingers began to undo her jacket and take it off.

'Very wise,' Joel murmured in soft satisfaction, watching her as he wandered over to the long, modern couch in the centre of the room. Suki put her coat over the back of a chair near the door, then forced herself to walk over to join him, every movement she made watched by sardonic eyes which observed the faint unsteadiness in her walk with apparent amusement.

'Sit down,' he said when she halted by the couch, and she reluctantly obeyed, running one shaky hand over the loose gleam of her red-gold hair. The rain had soaked through her scarf and she felt dampness under her fingers as she brushed her hair back from her face.

Joel handed her a glass. 'I don't like whisky,' Suki

protested, but took it, feeling the light brush of his fingers against her own as if she had touched fire, her hand jerking back, the amber-coloured liquid tilting violently in the glass.

'You're chilled and wet,' Joel said. 'You need it.' He sat down next to her, leaning back, his black head propped on one hand, his elbow supporting him as he faced her. Suki felt his knee touch hers and shot back involuntarily, trembling.

'Drink your whisky!' he ordered, and she lifted the glass and sipped, shuddering with distaste. The fiery liquid hit the back of her throat and began to spread through her veins while Suki stared at her own fingers clamped whitely around the glass.

'What is this place?' she asked, looking around the room and taking in the discreet, luxurious decor.

'Part of the Chairman's suite, we entertain here on occasions,' Joel answered, watching her. 'What were you really doing outside? And don't tell me you were meeting Richie Derby in the street—the idea's too fantastic. If you had a date with him you would have met him somewhere else.'

She finished the whisky and put the glass down on the leather-topped table beside them. 'I was walking. It started to rain and I ran under that overhang to shelter.'

'Rather a coincidence that you picked the head office of my company, isn't it?' Joel asked mockingly, and she was flushing.

'It was just a coincidence! I didn't even realise . . .'

'No?' he asked, his mouth curling in a maddening smile.

'No,' she insisted, but inside her head she was wondering if her feet had carried her there by pure chance or if, subconsciously, she had realised where she was walking. Joel Harlow had been very much on her mind, after all.

'I've got news for you,' said Joel after a moment's silence. 'It's on the cards that I'll be the next Chairman of Style,' he said softly, and Suki sat rigidly, stiffening, his tone warning her that he was expecting that announcement to shatter her, and was watching her like a hawk to see just how she would react. Suki was grateful for the advance warning Richie had given her—if she hadn't had that, she might have betrayed shock when Joel broke it to her.

She somehow managed to give him a cool look. 'Really? I didn't know you had any connection with them at all.'

She saw his eyes harden as though her calm response had annoyed him.

'I just bought a large block of shares from Sir Humphrey.'

'Oh? Why have you become interested in them?'

He surveyed her through heavy, guarded lids. 'Can't you guess?'

Colour ran up her face suddenly. 'If you think you can use them to browbeat me, you're wrong. You needn't have bothered. It won't work, Mr Harlow. You'll have wasted all your investment, I promise you.'

Joel's dark brows rose ironically. 'You flatter yourself, my dear Suki. Do you honestly believe I'd go to so much trouble just to blackmail you into bed?'

Biting her lip, she was forced to look away and

heard him laughing softly.

'Sorry to disillusion you,' he drawled. 'I flew to England for the express purpose of completing negotiations with Sir Humphrey, I'm afraid. This deal has been in the pipeline for weeks.' He flicked a long finger lightly down her cheek. 'You do jump to conclusions, don't you?'

'If I jumped to conclusions that's because you deliberately gave me the impression . . .' Suki stopped, too angry to finish that sentence. Joel moved closer, watching her intently and delicately winding one of her soft curls around his finger.

'What impression did I give you?' he asked, and she pushed his hand away.

'Leave my hair alone!'

'Your hair is an amazing colour,' he said, his eye moving over the cloudy mass of it. 'Fire and gold— every time you move your head, it glitters.' He looked into her eyes, smiling. 'I bought into Style for sound business reasons, but of course it does mean that I now have a very personal reason for taking an interest in your career.'

'I don't want you taking an interest in me or my career!'

'That's too bad,' he said calmly. 'Because I'm going to, and if you knew me better, Suki, you would know that issuing challenges like that was counter-productive. If I start a fight, I always win, as any number of people who've tried to take me on could tell you.'

She met his eyes and felt a strange little shiver running down her back. Maybe that was why he had become so determined in his pursuit of her, she thought, staring at the assertive, insistent face. He could not bear to be denied anything he wanted.

'I've always been fascinated by puzzles,' he explained. 'And you're a very complex puzzle, Suki.' He looked at her through his dark lashes and Suki shrank back, her breath caught painfully in the back of her throat.

'You have no right to harass me,' she muttered. 'I've told you no—why don't you just go away?'

'I told you—I never intend to say goodbye to you, Suki.' He put down his glass and his fingers closed round her chin, tilting her head back. Suki gave a tense gasp, trying to wriggle out of that hold, and his fingers became a steel vice that refused to release her. His other hand clamped her shoulder back against the couch, his long body poised above her, his thigh pinning her even more firmly under him.

'Let go of me!' She shoved at his wide shoulders and heard him laugh under his breath at her impotent little struggles.

The grey eyes gazed down into her own wide, terrified gaze. 'I'm not walking away from you and leaving it to some other man to unravel your mystery,' he told her with barbed mockery. 'I give you fair warning, Suki. I'm patient, persistent, ruthless in getting what I want.' His glance slowly moved down over the delicate modelling of her face until it focused on her trembling mouth. She drew a ragged breath as his head moved lower, slowly approaching, while she stared in dazed compulsion at the firm line of his own mouth, seeing the sensuality in the lower lip with aching awareness.

Before it had reached her mouth she felt her lids closing weakly, her lips parting on a feverish sigh of expectation. Her hands curled into his shoulders and her body swayed slightly towards him.

When that mouth touched hers, her heart contracted inside her with painful pleasure, but the touch was brief, a light butterfly kiss, then Joel was gone, and incredulously she opened her eyes again to find him standing up by the couch, mockery in every line of him.

'I've got a board meeting waiting for me,' he said, eyeing her with satisfied irony. 'I'm afraid I have to go. Can I get you a car to take you home?'

Suki was so shattered she just sat there, staring at him, and he laughed as he walked to the door.

'I'll tell them to send one round for you. Goodbye for now, Suki.'

He went out, closing the door, and she couldn't move for several minutes, a seething fury pulsing inside her. He had been making fun of her and she felt two inches high, she felt like throwing her empty glass across the room and watching it smash and splinter against the door through which Joel had just strolled with such self-satisfied amusement.

She was still sitting there on the couch, struggling with her temper, when a well-groomed secretary in a dark suit came into the room and politely informed her that a car was waiting for her and would take her where-ever she liked. Suki slid into her jacket and walked out into the lift with a fixed, artificial smile. The car drove her to the underground car park and she picked up her own car and drove back to Essex at a speed which would have horrified Buddy and Rosie if they had seen her. Suki was barely aware of her speed. Her mind was endlessly going over what Joel had said and always coming back with helpless rage to the moment when she weakly began to yield to that beautiful, sexy mouth only to find herself alone a second later while Joel Harlow walked away laughing. That had amused him, hadn't it?

She stepped ferociously on the accelerator and the car zoomed away past a long line of slow moving traffic whose drivers stared after her in rage as the low white car flashed out of sight. Suki barely noticed them. All she could think about was her own feelings of fury and humiliation. Why had he done it? The intense sting of rejection burned in her throat.

All her life, the bitter shadow of rejection had haunted her. It was the emotion to which she was most sensitive, the one thing which could cut through all her defences and drive her crazy.

It would be a long, long time before she recovered from what Joel had just done to her.

CHAPTER SEVEN

IT was all over the papers two days later, and Buddy was in a state of excited tension as he read the financial pages, trying to work out if Joel's bid for control of the company was good or bad as far as Suki's career was concerned. 'The question is—will he do a deal over the contract?' he thought aloud, and Suki caught the quick, secret look he gave her. It wasn't hard to decipher what that look meant. Buddy was remembering the distinct interest Joel had shown in her and wondering how he could use it in his fight to negotiate a better contract.

He got up casually and strolled off without saying anything more, but Rosie gazed after him wryly.

'Now what's he up to?' she enquired aloud of nobody in particular. Rosie knew every hair on Buddy's head and could guess his every move in advance. 'How am I ever going to leave him to his own devices?' she asked Suki a moment later. 'If I let him out of my sight, heaven alone knows what he'll get up to. After fifteen years with Buddy, a baby will be a piece of cake.'

'Are you getting used to the idea now?' Suki asked her, and Rosie gave a wry little shrug.

'Have I got a choice?'

Suki was going off to rehearsal in London that morning and Rosie decided to come with her to do some shopping. They drove into town in Suki's car and several times she caught Rosie staring absently after some young mother with a pram, her eyes reflective. 'You know, Suki,' Rosie murmured suddenly, 'I want this baby.'

Suki smiled, her eyes on the road. 'Of course you do.'

'I didn't think I did at first, but then I thought— it's my last chance, and that changed everything some- how. My only worry now is what I'm going to do about Buddy.'

'He's delighted about it!'

'Oh, I know that, that wasn't what I meant. But we've always done everything together, I've helped him build the business up from the ground floor— Buddy doesn't stir without me, you know that. How is he going to take it when I'm not around all day? He'll be like a lost dog.'

'He'll get used to it, and anyway, you won't opt out of everything, will you?'

'I've been thinking about that,' Rosie said rather defiantly, her face flushed. 'Well, when you come down to it, you only have those first years once, you can't go back and do it all again later. I think I ought to be around all day until the baby's school age. I don't fancy leaving my kid to someone else to bring up. If I'm going to have all the trouble of having it, I might as well get all the fun of watching it grow up, too.'

'Good for you,' said Suki softly, smiling. 'I couldn't agree more. I'd do the same, if it was me.'

'But how do I break it to Buddy?' Rosie asked, sighing. 'He has some idea I'll get a nanny and keep working, the same as I always have.'

'Don't break it to him,' Suki advised. 'Just let it

dawn on him gradually. I wouldn't be surprised if he didn't suggest it to you sooner or later.'

'He's getting quite possessive about the baby,' Rosie agreed, her nose wrinkling with amusement. 'Last night in bed he was making lists and I thought they were song titles for you, but when I looked at them do you know what they were? Lists of names.' She grinned. 'All boys' names, by the way. If it's a girl, Buddy will want his money back!'

Suki was worn out by the time she and Rosie drove back home that evening. She had been hard at work all day; her back ached, her feet ached, her head ached. 'I'm hoarse,' she told Rosie glumly. 'I could *not* hit that high note—I told Louis I'd never make it, but he insisted I could if I tried. Why is he so pigheaded?'

'Louis is a perfectionist, he doesn't like admitting you can't do everything he wants.'

'I wouldn't mind if he could sing a note, but he's the worst singer I ever heard,' Suki sighed.

'He can't be as bad as Buddy in the bath,' Rosie argued. 'Now Buddy always sounds like water going down a plughole.'

Suki yawned, stretching her jean-clad legs out as they waited in a line of homebound traffic for some lights to change. 'I am dead,' she groaned.

It was a blinding shock to her when she walked into the lounge half an hour later, her hands in her jacket pockets, to find Joel casually sprawled on the couch, watching her with ironic amusement as she halted in mid-step to stare at him.

Buddy was sitting opposite in one of the chairs, nursing a glass of whisky and looking furtive. Rosie followed hard on Suki's heels and shot Buddy a look of grim menace.

'Good evening,' Joel drawled. Suki gave him a brief nod and Rosie said: 'Good evening, Mr Harlow, how are you?' She switched her eyes to Buddy and smiled very sweetly. 'Could I have a word, sweetheart?'

Buddy had a shifty smile. 'Later, darling,' he promised, and Rosie said: 'Could you make that now, honey lamb?'

Buddy reluctantly got up, giving Joel a false grin. 'Excuse us for a minute, will you, Joel? Back in a flash.' He went out and Rosie very quietly closed the door. Suki and Joel stared at each other across the room.

'Let me get you a drink,' he said, rising.

'I'm just going to have a bath and change,' Suki said tersely, turning away.

'I want to talk to you,' said Joel, and she kept going, pretending she hadn't heard that. 'Now!' he said in a voice like a lash, and Suki stopped dead.

He moved over to the drinks cabinet and poured her a small gin and orange, came back and handed it to her. Suki had stripped off her jacket and with the glass in her hand sat down in the chair Buddy had vacated.

Joel stood in front of her chair, his hands in his pockets, his eyes half-sheathed by those heavy lids, surveying her with close attention. 'You look terrible,' he said curtly, and she gave him a furious look.

'Thank you, that's nice to know.' He looked maddeningly good; that lean body at ease in a polo-necked black sweater and tight black jeans which gave him a smouldering sexuality Suki found extremely disturbing. She knew she was tired, her face pale, her hair a tangled, windblown mess, but she wasn't exactly delighted to be told as much.

'I've just been telling Buddy,' said Joel. 'You need a long holiday.'

'I'm going to have one.'

'Yes,' Joel said. 'Next week you're flying out to the Bahamas.'

Her hand curled round the glass in surprise. She stared back at him, mouth open. 'When was this decided? And who by?'

'Ten minutes ago,' Joel told her. 'By me.'

'Now look,' Suki started and he cut her short with a hard, derisive smile.

'Don't argue, you're going. If you don't stop soon you'll just fold up on the pavement one day. I've never seen a stronger candidate for a nervous break-down.'

'Oh, don't be absurd,' she protested. 'I can't go yet—I've got any number of engagements fixed, I can't just back out of them.'

'You can and will, all you have to do is what you're told, leave the cancellations to Buddy.'

'I'll do nothing of the sort! Who do you think you are . . .'

'You'll be staying in Sir Humphrey's villa and you won't have to worry about a thing,' he said, ignoring her.

'I'm not just dropping everything and rushing off because you tell me to!'

'That's precisely what you're doing.'

'Do you know what you are? You're an egomaniac!' Suki told him in a voice hissing with rage.

'You'll fly there next Sunday,' Joel said with un-moved calm.

'I will not!' snapped Suki, longing to lift her glass and fling the gin at him.

'For two weeks all you'll do is lie on a beach and listen to the sound of the waves.' Joel gave her a mocking grin. 'Now isn't that a tempting thought? Sunshine, sea and sand—and absolutely nothing to do but enjoy them.'

'I can't cancel my engagements at such short notice, it isn't fair to people.'

'Suki,' Joel said softly through barely parted lips, and she looked up at him with wary attention.

'Yes?'

'Shut up,' he said.

Her lips parted to hurl back insults at him, she trembled with impotent fury at the calm authority of that tone, but as her eyes clashed with those grey ones she bit her lip and was silent, not quite daring to say anything.

'That's better,' Joel said with satisfaction.

'What gives you the idea you can dictate my life to me? I'm not your possession . . .'

'Not yet.'

'Not ever, don't kid yourself,' Suki spat, glaring at him. 'I'll take a holiday when it suits me.'

'You'll take one now before you crack up.' She opened her mouth to snap back and he held up a hand. 'And before you say whatever's burning on the end of your tongue, let me point out that you are a company asset and it is in the interests of Style to make quite sure that you don't fall to pieces next month. I've been talking to your maid and . . .'

'Maid?' Suki broke in, frowning.

'What's her name? Tilly?'

'Milly,' Suki said on a long-suffering sigh. 'I might have known! She's got some bee in her bonnet about me being overworked. If the truth were known, it's Milly who needs a holiday. She just uses me as an excuse.'

Joel rocked on his heels, those wide shoulders fitting smoothly under the thick black sweater. 'God almighty, you're a blinkered female!'

Suki looked at him, green eyes flashing. 'Don't you swear at me! I get enough of that when I'm working.'

'Do you ever look in a mirror?' he demanded.

'Too often,' Suki said. 'My appearance is part of my stock-in-trade, or hadn't you realised that?'

There was an alteration in the hard-boned face, a softening, a teasing mockery. 'Oh, I'd noticed,' he said in a slow, warm voice. 'I have hardly thought of anything else since the day I met you.'

Hot colour crawled up her face and she sprang out of her chair to flee. Laughing, Joel caught her by the waist and she struggled, glaring at him.

'Get your hands off me! How many times do I have to tell you . . .'

'Now you look alive!' Joel told her, staring down into her furious face. 'But most of the time you look as if you've been run over by a steamroller. You can't go on day after day using up every ounce of energy and never putting any back, Suki. I want you to promise me you'll take at least two weeks off.'

She stood in the firm circle of his arms, her eyes down, thinking. His hands tightened as if he would like to shake her and she looked up, nodding. She might have argued but she knew he was making sense.

'Yes?' he asked, and she said: 'Yes,' her voice sulky.

He didn't release her. She felt one hand softly moving against her back, moulding and fondling her without urgency, the warm pressure rather comforting. 'There's a lot of the child in you, isn't there?' he said thoughtfully. 'That's why your business manager can run your life for you, that's why you've accepted this cosy set-up here. It makes you feel safe and puts off the evil day when you have to face up to yourself as an adult. Most of us face up to it in our teens, but you ducked out on it, didn't you? What are you so afraid of? That you might get hurt?'

Suki looked away from the probing grey eyes, her neck stretched as she leaned away from him to avoid that stare. Joel bent forward and with a shock she felt his lips heatedly graze along her skin from the base of her throat to her ear. Trembling, she thrust at his chest, but he took no notice.

'I won't hurt you, Suki,' he promised, his warm mouth against her ear, exploring the delicate convolutions of it and making her shudder with angry, excited pleasure.

'Don't you like that?' he whispered, continuing his exploration behind her ear, and she wished she could honestly shout back that she didn't, but it would be a lie. She liked it, she wanted him to carry on with those gentle, seductive caresses which were so entirely new to her, because she had never allowed anyone to come this close before. Other men had tried and backed off in the face of her cold rejection, but Joel Harlow just kept on coming and she didn't know what to do about him. She didn't know what to do about herself and her weak-kneed desire to have him touch her. One part of her mind firmly insisted that it was insanity. Her career had always been enough for her in the past. She had given everything in her to building up her career and she had never once looked aside at anyone. But there was another part of her mind which had become rebellious, and that was bothering her very much.

Joel stroked back the windblown red-gold hair with one hand, brushing his lips across her eyes, closing them. She breathed rapidly, feeling his mouth on her flickering lashes.

'You take life too seriously,' he murmured. 'It's time you learnt how to play. Maybe that's what you've missed out on—I'll have to teach you how to enjoy life.'

He was teaching her now and she knew it. She should break away, put a stop to this before it went too far, but she couldn't bring herself to move.

Joel slid his lips down the taut plane of her flushed cheek and she kept her eyes shut, a heavy lethargy settling on her; a warm, languorous sensation centred on the movements of that mouth. She knew he was slowly advancing towards her lips and she could hear his heart beating faster, the deep heavy sound part of the spell he had woven around her. All her senses were fixed in attention to him and her mind was asleep, her body poised eagerly for the moment when his mouth reached her own.

When the door opened, they whirled apart, both of them flushed and breathless, shaken out of their deep awareness of each other by Rosie's arrival, the spell broken, shattered. Suki met Rosie's amused, curious look and couldn't stay in that room another second. She rushed past Rosie without a word and got to her own room with relief.

She flung herself on the bed, half sobbing, half laughing, torn between angry amusement and self-accusation. She couldn't even work out how she had come to let Joel coax her into such passive, helpless response. One minute they had been arguing, the next she had been in his arms letting him do exactly how he pleased.

Rosie's face! she thought, covering her eyes with her hands and twisting about on the bed in embarrassment. What had Rosie been thinking? After all her noisy protests, all her claims to find Joel Harlow irritating, she had been in his arms when Rosie walked in and it must have been obvious that she wasn't even struggling. Maybe it had been obvious that she hadn't even been a passive victim, she had been wrapped in pleasure by every successive caress.

It was some time before she slid off the bed and stripped to take a bath. She relaxed in the warm, scented water, her eyes closed, trying to forget those moments in Joel's arms, but furiously aware of the fact that every time she let her control of her mind slip the memory flooded back. She had never experienced a pleasure like it, and, however she might try to deny it to herself, she knew she craved a further demonstration of his ability to give pleasure.

Of course he knew how to seduce a woman, she told herself bitterly. Hadn't he had plenty of practice? He knew exactly what he was doing, the lingering sensual brush of his mouth hypnotic only because he had held so many other women in his arms. He was an expert in the field and once he had had what he wanted from her he would reject her, turn away, sated, forgetting her. She wanted the pleasure he could give her, but she knew she would die with the pain which must follow. It would kill her if she let herself love him and he got bored with her.

What had he said to her, after all? He had promised to teach her how to play, to enjoy life, but Suki knew that you can't change your nature, you can only meet life from your own angle of vision. Her whole life had taught her very different lessons about living from the ones Joel had learnt. Life might have been a playground to him. For Suki it had been a cold, grey, empty place.

That was the dream which troubled her whenever she was under stress. In that dream she was lost and alone in a grey tunnel, knowing that somewhere a brighter landscape existed but that she would never break through to it. She did not dream of monsters or threatening peril. She dreamt of nothing, of a dead chill emptiness, and she woke up shivering and needing light and music and voices to fill the aching void.

Getting out of the bath, she towelled herself absently, her eyes half seeing the smooth white gleam of her body as she wrapped the towel around her breasts and opened the door, the mirror throwing back that familiar image but showing her, too, the trembling curve of her mouth, the disturbed and feverish green eyes. It was revealed in her flesh, the impact Joel had made on her, and that angered her. He had got too close, and it was dangerous to her to let anybody get too close.

She dressed in a simple dark green skirt and white sweater and was sitting at her dressing-table doing her make-up when she heard the sound of a car, the engine note diminishing as it drove away. Her hand shook and she crossly got a grip on herself. Joel had gone, obviously, which was a relief, and she meant to take steps to erase him from her life in every way she could. She had had a serious alarm today. She didn't need a repeat performance, did she?

Buddy had a hangdog air when she joined him ten minutes later. He threw her a proprietorial smile. 'Hi, how did rehearsals go?'

'Don't ask. What was Joel Harlow doing here?'

'We were discussing your contract,' Buddy told her, sliding her a coaxing smile. 'By the way, he's won his boardroom battle, and he promised that when he gets back from the States in a few weeks he'll get down to serious consideration of your contract. Good news?'

'He's going back to the States?'

Buddy nodded. 'Flying tonight, apparently, but he assured me he would be over here again very soon.'

'Did he say anything else?' Suki told herself she was deeply relieved to hear Joel was leaving the country, wouldn't be around for a while, bothering her and disturbing her. It made her feel much better, she told herself, it lifted a weight from her shoulders and she was going to forget him. Thinking all that should have been very reassuring and she couldn't imagine why she felt faintly depressed, instead.

Buddy stared at her. 'What about?' Then he said: 'Oh, yes, he brought up the subject of your holiday—

Sir Humphrey's villa is at our disposal, he said, and he thought it was high time you took a few weeks off.'

'Interfering busybody,' Suki muttered.

'I said we'd jump at the offer,' Buddy told her. 'He's right, you need a break. Louis says your singing has gone ragged.'

'Oh, does he?'

'Your mind isn't on the job these days, Louis thinks. You can't concentrate properly and you keep missing on your timing and sliding off notes.'

Suki's teeth met. 'Louis has a lot to say for himself, doesn't he? Why didn't he say any of this to me today?'

'He's worried about you, we're all worried about you. A few weeks in the sun doing nothing and you'll be singing like a bird again. Oh, come on, Suki, you must know you've lost power, you're not singing at your peak these days. You worked full out for the concert and you gave us all you'd got, and it's left you drained. Ever since you've been walking about like a ghost.'

She felt like screaming at him that if she was looking unlike herself that was Joel Harlow's fault, but then she looked away, chewing on her lower lip angrily. It would be good to get away for a few weeks, she admitted to herself. Whatever the real reason, she had been feeling very odd over the last few weeks. Ever since the big concert, in fact, so maybe Buddy was right, maybe she had used up every spare ounce of energy on that night and perhaps what she needed was to stop dead for a while and do absolutely nothing.

'Agreed?' Buddy said shrewdly, watching her.

Suki sighed. 'Agreed.'

'That's my girl!' Buddy grinned, relaxing in his chair. 'Don't worry about your engagements—I'll cancel them all and make return dates where wanted. There's nothing urgent coming up, anyway, the recording can wait.'

Rosie tactfully said nothing about what she had seen when she walked in on Joel and Suki. Suki waited for some teasing comment, but none came. All that was occupying Rosie was the prospect of a holiday in the sun. Rosie was a sun-lover, she often said her idea of heaven was having absolutely nothing to do all day but lie in the sun. That made Suki laugh, because one thing you noticed about Rosie immediately was her energy, her light quick movements which got things done in half the time anyone else would take. When Rosie relaxed, though, she did so with the same determination she brought to everything else, because, she said, whatever you did you should do with everything you had got.

They were due to fly to the Bahamas on the Sunday morning of the following week and Milly spent all day Saturday packing for them. She had a genius for it—she could get more into a suitcase than you would ever have believed possible. Milly said it was years of experience, she had done it so many times she could do it in her sleep.

'You taking this?' she asked Suki, waving a chiffon negligee at her, and Suki shook her head.

'Just the little towelling robe—I told you.'

'Right,' said Milly, and gave her a look of grim satisfaction. 'Now you make sure you have a good holiday, you understand?'

'I'm going to, don't nag.'

'It's always those who need them who don't take them,' Milly said, deftly tucking a pile of silk undies into the case.

'Where are you going for your holiday?' Suki asked curiously, curled up on the bed with a pile of sheet music.

'Where I always go,' Milly said.

'Not Bournemouth again!' protested Suki, laughing and got an offended look.

'What's wrong with that? I like to have some peace and quiet when I'm on holiday.'

Buddy came into the room, frowning. 'Suki, you and Rosie are going to have to fly without me tomorrow—something's come up. I've got to stay in London for the next couple of days to see Richie Derby.'

Milly stopped packing and listened curiously. Suki lifted her eyebrows in quizzical surprise. 'Richie? Why are you seeing him? I thought you said you'd never even speak to him again after the way he walked out on you when he went to the States?'

'I can change my mind, can't I?' Buddy asked, grimacing. 'He's just been on the phone, he's quarrelled with his agent and he asked if I'd have him back. There's going to be a lot to sort out this end and I can't fly off and let it all wait until I come back, it might be too late by then. I'll get it done and join you as soon as I can, I promise.'

'Have you told Rosie?'

'Just now. She was livid,' said Buddy.

'I'm not surprised!'

'Look, Richie is a big catch, I can't turn my back

on the chance of getting him back. You know that in this business you have to seize every chance you get. Rosie knows that, too.' He grinned at Suki. 'With the baby coming we're going to need as much money as we can get.'

'That blessed baby's going to get blamed for everything,' Milly muttered, and Buddy threw her a scowl.

'Shut up, you old witch! How Suki puts up with you I'll never know. I'd turf you out on your ear if I was her.'

'No, you wouldn't, because I wouldn't work for you if you paid me ten times what I get now.' Milly gave him a tart look. 'Rosie has too much patience with you, that's your trouble. You've been spoilt. Some women wouldn't put up with you.'

'Meaning you, I suppose?'

'Oh, I wouldn't,' Milly nodded. 'Not in a million years.'

Suki lay listening to the old, familiar squabble between them, smiling. It meant nothing, they enjoyed brawling cheerfully, they loved swapping insults, it gave salt to their lives. Buddy had known Milly for many years, they had been brought up in the same district of London and had both moved in the same circles in show business, since Milly had worked for a succession of famous stars. That edgy banter between them was part of the family atmosphere which had made her feel so safe during the past five years. There was no real bite to their rows. Right from the start, listening to them had given Suki a glimpse of how it must be in a real family, something she had never known before, something she had longed to experience.

Buddy went out with Milly yapping at his heels like

a short-tempered terrier, and Suki stared at the ceiling, her face blank. It made her worried to realise how much things were changing around her. Life had seemed so settled and calm and safe until the night of that concert. Now she felt as though time had given a flick of the kaleidoscope of life and the pattern had altered, in a variety of ways. Joel's influence on her was only part of it. Rosie had changed—the approaching baby had acted on her in so many ways; her personality had softened, the wry cynicism was less in evidence lately. Suki could see that Rosie had less attention these days either for her or Buddy. Their little family was shifting, the axis altered. This house had rotated around Suki's existence until now, everyone in it absorbed in her career, but things would never be the same again.

Rosie had changed, Buddy had changed and Suki knew that she herself had changed too. She wasn't ready yet to explore the various tiny shifts of her mind. She leapt back mentally from the prospect, closing her eyes to it.

Next morning she woke up when her alarm clock shrilled, leapt out of bed at once and began to get ready, but when she left the room a quarter of an hour later she found Buddy huddled in a dressing-gown in the kitchen with a cup of black coffee and a sleepy face, with no sign of Rosie in evidence.

'Good morning,' Suki said brightly. 'Rosie not up yet?'

'She's feeling too ill to move,' Buddy said gloomily.

Suki stared at him. 'What's wrong?'

'The usual thing,' he muttered. 'I've rung the doctor —this morning sickness isn't getting any better and I don't like the look of her at all.'

Suki sat down, paling. 'You think something's really wrong?'

'I don't know, do I?' Buddy snapped. He looked over his shoulder at the window. 'Thank God, there's his car now—I wondered how long it was going to take him, I rang him an hour ago.' He got up and went out to let the doctor in, his voice deep and nervous and angry. Suki sat listening, her face alarmed. She heard them go upstairs, the opening and closing of a door. A pot of coffee stood on the kitchen table. Suki got herself a cup and poured some coffee, sat there, sipping it, her cold hands wrapped around the cup for warmth. Please God, there's nothing really wrong, she thought miserably. Rosie wanted this baby, she might have been horrified at the start, but now she was going to be badly hurt if anything went wrong with it. Her eyes fixed on the sunlight gleaming along the paths, the vivid golden trumpets of daffodils swaying in a light breeze, the whole garden bathed in spring sunlight. On a morning like this it was hard to contemplate the possibility that something could have gone wrong with Rosie's baby. Life could be very unfair, she thought angrily, then grimaced at the childish sound of that.

She stiffened, hearing the door upstairs opening, then the sound of footsteps on the stairs and voices. They sounded surprisingly cheerful, or was she imagining that? Buddy said loudly: 'Thank God for that!' and Suki heard the doctor answer in a lower voice. The front door was opened and closed and the sound of a car engine started. Buddy walked into the kitchen behind her. Suki looked at him sharply.

'Is she all right?'

'He says so,' Buddy told her in a much more cheerful voice. 'He takes it all very calmly, says some women have a problem at the start with morning sickness, but it will stop in a few weeks and all Rosie has to do is rest in bed for a while.'

'But she's going to be okay?' Suki insisted, and Buddy nodded with a reassuring smile.

'He said there's absolutely nothing wrong except that Rosie is forty years old and this is her first baby.' Buddy put a hand on the coffee pot. 'Is this still drinkable? I need a strong cup of coffee.' He poured one, then looked at Suki over the brim of the cup. 'I'm afraid the holiday is off, for Rosie, though. The doctor said no flying until she's settled down a bit.'

'Oh,' Suki said, then after a brief pause, 'Well, I won't go either, then,' and Buddy said sternly:

'Of course you will—don't be ridiculous. This holiday was for you, anyway. You're the one who really needs it and you're going. The car will be here in a minute, your cases are in the hall.'

'I can't go on holiday alone,' Suki protested.

'Why not? Everything's arranged. The car will take you to the airport, you fly to the Bahamas and a car will meet you there and take you to the villa. You're not afraid of getting lost en route, are you?' Buddy was being sarcastic, his voice teasing, but Suki was taken aback at the idea of going away alone for two weeks. She hadn't been anywhere over the past five years without one of them in attendance, and the idea of flying off on her own was something of a shock.

'You just have a good time,' said Buddy, watching

her. 'You'd better go up and see Rosie before you leave
—she's worried about you going off alone. Don't upset
her, will you?'

Suki got up. 'No,' she promised. 'It's a surprise,
that's all, I wasn't expecting to go alone.'

'You're a big girl now,' Buddy said. 'I think maybe
we'd all lost sight of the fact. We'd got used to you being
a scared kid that we didn't notice you growing up over
the years. We kept right on thinking of you as a
seventeen-year-old. Sooner or later this had to happen
—you've got to be pushed out of the nest for your own
good, Suki.'

She stood watching him, her face pale. 'Is that
what's happening? I'm being pushed out of the nest?'

'Just to try your wings for a while,' Buddy said,
smiling. 'Who knows? You may find you can fly perfectly well on your own and don't need us any more.'
He grimaced at her. 'Don't forget, though, I'm the best
business brains in show business, will you? I don't
want you to fly away too far.'

Suki went upstairs and found Rosie lying on her
pillows looking very pale. Opening her eyes, she looked
across the room and made a wry face. 'I'm sorry to
louse things up for you, Suki, but have a good holiday
and don't worry about a thing.'

'Are you sure . . .' Suki began, and Rosie interrupted, nodding.

'I want you to have this holiday and I'll be fine. I'm
not getting out of this bed again until the room stops
going around in circles. By the time you get back I
should be over the worst, according to the doctor. He
says everything's perfectly normal—normal, I ask you!

What a word to use.'

Suki laughed, relaxing slightly. Pale or not, Rosie was still herself, that wry light voice still determined to find fun even in being ill.

'Suki, the car's here!' Buddy yelled, and Suki went over to give Rosie a quick hug before she hurried out. Buddy kissed her and put her into the back of the chauffeur-driven car. She turned her head to wave at him, feeling oddly nervous and unsure of herself as she drove away. Not since she was seventeen had she been left to fend for herself, she realised, Buddy and Rosie had organised her whole life down to the very smallest detail and it would be surprising if her sense of adventure hadn't atrophied during the years of being wrapped in protective cottonwool. Just occasionally she had revolted to the extent of clearing out for an hour or two to drive around the narrow Essex roads in her car, but that had been a very minor rebellion and she had never made any attempt to evade the gentle tyranny to which she was subject.

As her plane rose into the bright, morning sky she looked down on the tiny toylike buildings disappearing far below her and felt a strange, nervous, excited tingle inside herself. It was ridiculous to feel as though today she had reached a watershed in her life, but she did; the conviction was growing inside her with every second that passed. She wasn't sure whether the change had begun to occur the night she met Joel or not, but she knew that there had been some change, both in herself and in her life, and that when she came back from the Bahamas she would be returning to a different way of life, as a different girl.

CHAPTER EIGHT

Suki lay on her stomach on an enormous yellow beach towel, a white straw hat over her hair, the fringed brim shading her nape from the heat of the sun, a striped beach umbrella fluttering gently above her. Behind her she could hear the soft whisper of the waves creaming over the sand and a seabird giving a harsh call as it divebombed the blue sea.

Within reach of her hand lay a paperback thriller she had bought at Heathrow but which she had never managed to finish reading because she couldn't keep her mind on it for more than a few pages at a time. Beside it stood a bottle of suntan lotion which she had just finished smoothing into her skin.

She had been here for four days now and she had sunbathed every day, taking care not to overdo it at first but gradually accustoming her skin to the strong sunlight of the island. She had already gone through the stage of turning pink, but she hoped now to start acquiring an overall tan. The little private beach led down from the villa gardens and she could just see the white walls of the sprawling building through a closely set thicket of luxuriant glossy-leaved trees.

At intervals along the coast other villas were dotted, she knew, from the drive to the villa on the day of her arrival, when the smiling dark-skinned chauffeur had insisted on pointing out every one to her and telling her at length who lived in them. This part of the island was, she gathered, very exclusive and expensive to live in and nearly all the villas belonged to rich people who only used them at intervals or lent them to their friends. Suki had been very tired after her flight and she had leaned back, only half listening, as the man gave her a rapid guide to the local beauty spots en route for Sir Humphrey's villa.

She already knew that it was staffed by local people who would be there to welcome her, but from the driver she discovered that the staff actually lived in the villa in a separate wing. He even knew their names and when Suki climbed out of his car in front of the rambling building she was able to pick out the white-haired man greeting her at once and use his name, smiling. 'You must be FitzGerald,' she had said, and he had given her a solemn inclination of the head and replied: 'That is correct, miss,' so much in the style of an English butler in some old film that Suki had trouble stifling a smile. She did suppress it, however, which was fortunate, she realised later, because FitzGerald would not have been amused. He took himself and his position in the villa very seriously indeed and expected everyone else to do so. Tall, stately, with intelligent dark eyes which missed nothing, FitzGerald would have been most at home in some diplomatic post where his talents would have had a chance to shine at their best. He was, Suki felt, wasted as the major-domo of Sir Humphrey's villa.

Nothing was beyond him. He anticipated her every wish and ran the villa like clockwork, his rule never questioned by the other servants, who treated him with far more respect than Suki could ever remember seeing anyone treat Sir Humphrey. Suki merely had to mention that she liked shellfish for the most delicious varieties of it to appear on her lunchtable. After the first morning, when she was served a large breakfast she barely touched, she found herself offered only fruit and fruit juices for breakfast. FitzGerald didn't miss a thing, and he did not need to be reminded about anything, either. Any item of food Suki did not particularly like was never served again, even if she hadn't expressed her dislike. She thought, at times, that FitzGerald plucked her thoughts out of the air.

'How long have you worked here, FitzGerald?' she asked him once, and he looked courteously bland as he said he had been with the villa for twenty years.

'Has Sir Humphrey owned it as long as that?' Suki enquired, rather surprised.

'Sir Humphrey acquired the villa four years ago,' FitzGerald informed her.

'Who had it before that?'

'A gentleman from America,' FitzGerald said. 'We saw very little of him and he sold the villa again within a year.' He moved back from the table, ending the conversation with polite firmness by vanishing. He was very far from being a gossip and, however courteous, did not encourage Suki to open conversations with him. She got the feeling that FitzGerald regarded the villa as a very special private hotel with himself as a hotel manager. He might have something, she thought. Clearly, Sir Humphrey rarely came here, but was casual about lending the place to friends and business acquaintances, and there was a curiously unreal air about the place. It was always immaculately tidy, but despite the luxurious furniture and decor, it gave her an uncomfortable feeling. She could relax far more easily out here on the beach and preferred to spend most of her time out of the villa, finding it hard to feel at home in the silent empty rooms, her occupation of the house defensive, wary, leaving as little trace of her presence as she could.

By throwing her back on her own company it was forcing her to think too much and she did not want to think at all. She had done too much of that lately and when things are changing around you there is a strong instinct to hold your ground, dig your heels in and refuse to budge, either physically or mentally, until you can feel secure again.

Eyes closed, Suki felt the sun pouring down on her. She had undone the strings of her bikini top so that she could get a smooth tan on her back and in another moment or two, she decided, she would turn over before her skin started to overheat.

The sound of feet churning up the pale powdery sand startled her. She shifted on to one elbow, peering round the umbrella, and stared in disbelief at the young man walking towards her.

He grinned. 'Surprise, surprise!'

'Richie! What on earth . . .'

'I just flew in, and I've got a message from your sponsor,' he said, reaching her and flinging himself down on the sand beside her. 'Buddy says if you're not having a good time and enjoying yourself he'll stop your pocket money.'

She sat up, holding the loose cups of her bikini top

in place with both hands while Richie eyed her admiringly. 'I was talking to him on the phone a couple of days ago and he didn't mention you were coming.'

'I only decided yesterday.'

'What are you doing here?'

'Same as you, darling, having a holiday.'

She looked at him with faint wariness. 'Here?' Her glance moved to the villa and Richie laughed.

'No, I'm staying at a hotel.' He gave her a wicked, teasing look. 'Although, if you invited me . . .'

Suki smiled but ignored the teasing remark. 'When did you get here?'

'This morning.' He stretched out beside her with a long sigh, his blond hair spilling over the sand, his slim body already pale tan. He was wearing a pair of brief blue shorts and a short-sleeved white cotton shirt which he had unbuttoned so that it fell back open from his smooth-skinned chest. 'Hey, this is a great place, I could have a ball here,' he said. 'You renting it for long?'

'A few weeks. Did Buddy say if Rosie was okay, by the way?'

'That was the other message,' he agreed. 'You're not to worry, she's fine, out of bed and giving Buddy a headache—everything's as normal, he said.'

She gave a sigh of relief. 'That's good, I was worrying about her.'

Richie turned over on to his side, propping up his head with one hand, the sun glinting on the fine silky strands of his hair, which tumbled forward over his fingers as he did so. 'I can't get over the idea of Rosie having a baby. Who'd have thought it? I used to get the feeling she wasn't the domesticated type and it was she who ran the firm, not Buddy.'

'Between you and me, there's a lot in that idea,' Suki told him. 'Rosie has a very good business head. But both she and Buddy are delighted about the baby.'

'Yeah, I could see Buddy was tickled pink.'

'Have you signed up with him again, by the way?'

'More or less, but first he's got to sort out a legal tangle with my ex-agent.' A discontented expression crossed his fair-skinned face. 'I wouldn't trust that guy farther than I could throw him—I'll be glad to get rid of him. He's a real shark!'

'What did you quarrel about?'

'What do you think? Money, what else? Sometimes I hate the stuff—it brings out the worst in everyone.'

'At least you know you can trust Buddy where money's concerned.'

'That's why I've gone back to him,' Richie agreed.

Suki was getting tired of holding her bikini top in place. She held it with one hand while she tried to clip it together at the back with the other and Richie grinned at her, kneeling up.

'Turn round, I'll do it.'

She turned and felt his fingers grasp the thin strap. 'How long are you staying here?'

'We haven't made up our minds.' He clipped the two halves of the strap and patted her lightly on her rear. 'There you go, sweetheart.'

She looked at him over her shoulder. 'We?'

'I'm with my little lady,' he said, and Suki lifted an eyebrow.

'Are you married, Richie?'

'Not so you'd notice,' he said, then grinned at her. 'It might happen one day. We've been together for six months and it's still all systems go, so who knows? I don't believe in rushing things, but she's something pretty special and I wouldn't want to lose her.'

'Don't you,' Suki said soberly. 'I'd like to meet her.'

'She'd like to meet you,' said Richie. 'I'd have brought her this morning, but Buddy said you were resting and I wasn't to break in on you for long, so Annette stayed at the hotel. She's a fan of yours—got all your records, drives me potty playing them night and day.'

'That's nice,' Suki said, smiling. 'I sang a couple of your songs at my concert, you know, I'm a fan of yours.'

'Mutual admiration society,' he said, getting up. 'I like it.'

Richie's boyish blond looks were deceptive. He was clever and shrewd under that little boy look. You only had to listen to his songs to know that, beneath the simplicity of the words and music ran a vein of poetry which didn't intrude on the surface but was there if you looked for it.

Suki got up too, collecting her lotion and the paperback book, her towel and sunglasses. 'I'll walk back up to the house with you.'

Richie slid a casual arm around her bare sunwarmed waist, his fingers lightly splayed across her midriff. 'What do you say to a little get-together at our hotel tomorrow night?'

'Lovely, I'd like that.'

He smiled at her. 'Great. Annette will be over the

moon at the prospect of meeting you.'

'What does Annette do? Is she in the music business too?'

'No, she's a lawyer,' said Richie, and Suki did a double-take, her eyes opening wide in disbelief.

'You're having me on!'

He laughed. 'No, it's a fact. She works for a New York firm. She's very bright. There's more to Annette than a pretty face—and it is pretty, take it from me. Annette's stunning. I keep thinking I know everything to know about her and then I find out I'm wrong, she still has a new angle I haven't met before.'

'She sounds like a clever lady,' Suki commented, amused. It sounded as though Annette was either an exceptional person or a girl who knew how to keep pulling surprises out of a hat.

'I've never known anyone like her,' Richie went on, a faintly dreamy look on his face.

They were walking slowly through the beautifully landscaped, well-kept gardens surrounding the villa, and as they reached the verandah Suki halted and smiled at him. 'I'll look forward to meeting her.'

'Dinner tomorrow, then? They have a floor show and dancing at the hotel in the evenings. We can make a night of it.'

'I'll enjoy that,' said Suki. and got a shrewd look.

'Getting bored, Suki?'

'Just the tiniest bit,' she admitted with a little grimace, and Richie glanced around them, faint irony in his face.

'Nice place to get bored in, though. I'd have thought you needed a holiday away from it all. Pretty hectic life you lead, isn't it? Buddy was telling me you've been working yourself to a standstill.'

'You didn't happen to notice his slavedriver's whip while he was saying that, I suppose?' enquired Suki drily, and Richie laughed.

'Shall I pick you up tomorrow or can you make your own way to the hotel?'

'I'll drive in,' she said.

'See you, then,' he told her, turning away and walking off with lithe, rapid steps. She watched him follow the path around the villa to the front drive. His car started and drove away, then Suki went into the cool shadowy lounge, her towel swinging from her hand as she clacked over the tiled floor to the bathroom. Although she had been enjoying her peaceful days in the sun she was rather pleased to have an interruption and she was looking forward to the next evening. Richie was an undemanding, lively companion, and his lady sounded interesting. Suki was glad they had turned up. It had been kind of Buddy to suggest Richie dropped in on her, and typical of him. Buddy was always thoughtful, generous, a man who, however busy he might be, somehow managed to spare time for the small courtesies which make life so much happier for everyone.

Annette was even more of a surprise than Richie had hinted—she turned out to be a tiny, bubbly blonde with huge blue eyes which sparkled like the sea with the sun dancing across it. The last thing Suki would have suspected, had she met her without knowing anything about her, was that Annette was a lawyer, but, as she talked to her that evening, her initial disbelief faded and she was very impressed by the shrewd mind behind that lively face.

The hotel was a large white modern building which was only half full at this end of the season and when, after dinner, the local band began to play there were only a few couples drifting around the floor to the music.

'You'll have to share me between you,' Richie said complacently, grinning at them. 'No fighting over me, girls!'

Annette glanced at Suki drily. 'Fancies himself, doesn't he?'

'How can you say that?' Richie asked in dulcet tones. 'I'm the most modest guy you ever met, you know that.'

Annette stood up. 'I'm going to the cloakroom, so Suki can have the first dance.' She winked at Suki. 'Watch your toes—he dances like an elephant!'

Richie hooted protestingly as she walked away, but his amused eyes followed her until she was lost to sight before he turned, getting up, and held out a hand to Suki.

She was feeling oddly lonely. The banter and teasing between Richie and Annette made her feel rather left out. It was never much fun to be the third in company with an obvious pair, and the other two were so wrapped up in each other that even though they kept remembering to bring her into their talk Suki couldn't help realising that what they really wanted was to be alone.

'What do you think of her?' Richie asked eagerly. 'Isn't she fantastic?'

'I like her very much,' Suki told him soberly. 'You're

very lucky, Richie, and you're right—she is something special.' Annette was lucky, too, she thought, because Richie was a very nice guy and he, too, combined looks with intelligence. They were a well matched pair, and Suki envied them the warm happiness you could almost almost see as they talked together, laughed, danced, argued together.

'We'll be seeing you,' Richie promised as they put her into her car later that evening.

'Drop in any time you're at a loose end,' Suki said, smiling at them both. She did not expect to see them again, of course. It had been nice of them to spare an evening from their dream holiday and she didn't blame them if they preferred to spend all their time together.

That evening as she stood at her bedroom window staring out at the deep, deep blue of the night sky she felt very conscious of her loneliness. She was afraid to go to sleep because she dreaded the arrival of the grey dream which had haunted her all her life. Being an observer of Richie's happiness with Annette had underlined for her the hollow nature of the success for which she had worked so hard, for which she had sacrificed everything else. Lately she had begun to ask herself if the threat of the dream had not already come true— had she locked herself into that loneliness long ago? Some fears can be self-fulfilling. If you try to guard against something you fear you can actually set in motion the circumstances which bring about the very thing you dread. Was that what she had done?

By running from any possibility of being hurt by rejection, was she rejecting life itself? She shivered, turning away, and climbed into bed, flinching away from any further thought which might disturb her even more.

Two days later while she was sunbathing on the beach Richie strolled down to greet her, his skin already tanned a smooth pale gold. She sat up, smiling. 'Hallo, where did you spring from? Where's Annette?'

'At the beauty parlour having her hair done,' said Richie, glancing over the vivid blue of the sea. 'I just called in to ask how you were and see if you'd like to come over to the hotel to catch the floor show on our last night. We're flying back to the States in a couple of days.'

'That's very nice of you, I'd enjoy it,' Suki said. 'But are you sure you wouldn't rather spend your last night together?'

'We thought of making it a kind of celebration,' Richie explained, grinning. 'We decided to get married and we'd like you to be the first to know.'

Suki laughed, delighted by the news. 'That's wonderful! I'm very happy for both of you, and I'm sure you're going to be very happy together.'

'I'm sure we are,' Richie agreed. 'So you'll come?'

'I'd love to.'

She got up, collecting her various possessions and they walked up to the villa together, Richie's arm lightly round her waist as he strolled beside her talking excitedly about his plans. 'Annette's keeping her career going for the moment, but she wants to start a family next year. It's because we want children that we're getting married. It will be marvellous for me to have a real, settled home again. That's what I've missed since I went to the States.'

Suki listened, glancing at the villa, then did a double-take, her eyes dazzled by the strong sunlight for a few seconds into wondering if she was seeing things. Then she stared hard and knew she wasn't imagining anything. The tall figure leaning against one of the white columns was there, and it *was* Joel Harlow.

Richie hadn't noticed him yet. He was too busy talking about Annette, but he broke off suddenly, his mouth open in surprise as his eye touched on the poised and dangerous threat Joel somehow radiated as he watched them. It was absurd to imagine he threatened them, Suki told herself nervously, but she did feel it; she could almost see it, an air of menace surrounding Joel like an almost tangible halo.

'Well, hi,' said Richie, coming to a halt as they reached the verandah. He looked at Suki, who struggled to make her face stay calm. Richie looked back at the man facing them. 'Joel Harlow, isn't it? We met last year in New York. I don't know if you remember.' Richie was rather nervous, too, his voice very polite and careful. Joel Harlow was a powerful man.

'I remember,' Joel said, and Suki was reminded of the first time they met, that feeling she had had that this man was as cold as the Northern Lights, his eyes frosty and sharp and clear.

'I didn't know you were staying here,' Joel added, sweeping his chill stare from Richie to Suki and back again.

'Yes, I've been here for a few days,' Richie answered with a faint bewilderment at the atmosphere. He paused. 'Are you on holiday too, Mr Harlow?'

'Yes,' Joel said succinctly.

'Fantastic spot for a holiday,' Richie offered in a placatory voice, the voice of someone who knows he is meeting grim hostility but can't for the life of him fathom why.

'Yes,' said Joel, yet somehow he managed to convey an icy disagreement which Richie heard but couldn't interpret. Suki felt the uneasy look Richie gave her but deliberately avoided meeting it.

'We've been exploring the island,' Richie gabbled nervously. 'Driving around, taking a boat out, skin-diving—the usual tourist things.'

Joel nodded, his face as hard as flint, watching Richie in a way that reminded Suki of a matador confronting a bull. His glance slid down to where Richie's fingers lay across Suki's bare midriff and Richie almost snatched his hand away and looked at his watch with a show of surprise.

'Good heavens, look at the time! Nearly lunchtime.' He gave Joel a worried, false smile. 'I'm staying at the new hotel in town and they do a terrific range of seafood dishes. Do you like seafood, Mr Harlow?'

Joel said: 'Not particularly. Were you planning to have lunch here this morning?'

The words were perfectly courteous, but the tone in which they were delivered had the edge of an ice-axe and the hard lines of his face as he asked the question, the flinty grey eyes which chipped their way through Richie's startled gaze, made the question one which not only demanded, but expected, a negative answer. Only a brave or determined man would have said yes, and Richie hurriedly backed off from the challenge.

'No, no,' he said. 'I'm expected back at the hotel for lunch.' He gave Suki an alarmed, curious look. 'See you, Suki, I'll give you a ring about tomorrow night.'

'Yes, okay,' she said, but she said it to his vanishing back as Richie fled. In the silence she heard the slam of a car door, then the throb of an engine and a car drove away, the wheels grating on the drive in front of the villa.

Glaring at Joel accusingly, she broke out: 'What do you mean, talking to him like that? Why were you so unfriendly?'

'What was he doing here?' Joel demanded in turn as though he had every right to expect an answer.

'Richie's an old friend, someone I've worked with often, and he's a very nice guy.' She took a deep breath, vibrating with fury. 'Anyway, what are *you* doing here?'

'What do you mean—an old friend?' he asked, ignoring her own question. 'How well do you know him? Do you know, for instance, that he's been having a long affair with some pretty little blonde for the past six months?'

'So what?' Suki shrugged, and Joel looked at her with dangerous grey eyes.

'So what? Don't you care if you're breaking up someone else's life?'

'I'm not doing anything of the sort, it's nothing to do with me what Richie does or with whom.'

'I thought you said you didn't go in for love affairs,' Joel ground out, taking a step towards her, his hands curled at his sides as though he wanted to hit her. 'Why pick on a specimen like Richie Derby?'

'I like Richie,' she said, evading the point. Let him think what he liked. He had no right to stand there looking at her with distaste and biting condemnation when he didn't have any evidence except the sight of her with Richie. Her answer inflamed his temper, she could see that. Little flecks of red had invaded his hard-boned face and he seemed to be struggling with an incipient explosion, breathing in a harsh, rapid way which was very alarming.

She would have walked past him into the villa, but out here there was less danger of any of the servants eavesdropping on their quarrel, so she took the fight into the enemy camp in a sudden fit of reckless temper.

'Anyway, I'm on holiday, why shouldn't I amuse myself?' she asked him, and if she had wanted to foment the simmering rage inside him she certainly succeeded, because he took a long, hard breath, his eyes becoming deadly.

'So that's what you were doing, is it?' he asked, and she felt a peculiar trembling in the pit of her stomach at the tone of his voice. It sent a warning signal to her brain, but Suki ignored it, refused to let herself be intimidated by those icy grey eyes.

'Why shouldn't I? You told me yourself that it was time I learnt how to play,' she flung back deliberately. 'You were the one who said I ought to start having fun. You said I took life too seriously.'

'I said too damned much!' Joel erupted, and she felt her nerves jerk at the savage snarl of his tone.

FitzGerald appeared at the open, sliding window leading on to the verandah, his face calm and untroubled. 'Lunch is ready, Mr Harlow, sir,' he said in his most diplomatic voice, and Suki saw Joel pulling a stiff mask over his face before he turned his head towards the window.

'Thank you, FitzGerald, we'll be in directly.'

FitzGerald inclined his head and vanished again.

'Who asked you to lunch?' Suki demanded.

'I did,' said Joel, swivelling that black head back her way and giving her the sort of look which is longing for an argument.

Suki gave him what he seemed to want. 'You've got a nerve,' she said. 'It's usual to wait for an invitation before calmly announcing that you're staying for lunch.'

'I'm staying full stop,' said Joel, turning and walking into the house.

She pursued him, trembling with anger and alarm. 'What's that supposed to mean?'

He didn't wait for her. He kept on going, taking long strides which meant she had to almost run to catch up with him.

'I'm staying at the villa, too,' he said when she did, and Suki fizzed with helpless, incoherent fury.

'Who said? What do you mean, you're staying here too? You can't do that! Who invited you?'

'I did,' he said again with a species of satisfied malice which sent a wave of hot blood to her head.

'Sir Humphrey . . .' she began, and Joel turned his head to give her a smile like a knife.

'Doesn't own the villa any more.'

Suki stopped dead, staring at him, guessing, fuming, and Joel paused too, curving one sardonic brow above the gleam of his eyes.

'He sold it to you,' she said at last, and he nodded.

'Shrewd of you to leap to the right conclusion so fast.' That was spiky mockery and Suki could have hit him. He was getting his own back for the needling she had given him a few moments ago, and she could make a few more guesses which she suspected would be equally accurate and equally worrying. Joel had bought the villa deliberately, planned to get her here deliberately. He had erected a luxury trap for her and she had blindly walked straight into it.

'You're a . . .' she began in a husky, quavering voice, and he leant over and put one long finger lightly on her trembling lips, silencing the rest of that sentence.

'Naughty, mustn't use words like that!'

He took the finger away without hurrying, sliding it smoothly along her mouth, and as he walked away Suki hurled the word at his back like a dagger. 'Bastard!'

He stopped in his tracks, but she was already on her way to her bedroom, her sandals slapping on the cool, tiled floor. She slammed the door behind her and stood there, breathing fast, wondering what to do about this situation. After a long moment she walked into the shower and hurriedly stripped off before turning on the jet of water and letting the spray sluice over her sunwarmed body.

Grabbing the towel hanging ready by the sliding door, she dried herself, biting her lip, as she considered the implicit threat of Joel's presence at the villa. She could pack and leave, she thought, join Richie and his lady at the hotel a couple of miles away.

That would be the most sensible thing to do, but she had an uneasy suspicion she would have a hard time getting out of the neat little trap Joel had set for her. She couldn't walk to the hotel. She would need a car, and Joel might try to stop her getting one.

She dressed slowly in a brief green dress with an off-the-shoulder neckline. Her skin was hot after the hours in the sun and she found it easier to leave her shoulders bare. She did not bother to put on any make-up; the smooth pale gold of her skin looked good without any now. She brushed her loose red-gold hair until it was quite dry, framing her face with delicate curling tendrils which emphasised the vulnerable pale curve of her throat.

She was about to walk out of the bedroom when her eye fell on the white telephone by her bed, and her glance brightened. She hurried over to it and picked it up, but there was no response. A frown flicked over her face. She clicked the steel supports up and down. Nothing happened; the phone was dead. Slowly she replaced it, thinking hard. Was that a coincidence?

She went out and found Joel in the dining-room with FitzGerald, whose impassive face gave her no clue as to what they had been saying before she entered. Bowing slightly, FitzGerald began to pull back a chair for her and Suki looked at him sharply.

'The phone seems to be out of order,' she said.

FitzGerald didn't show a thing. 'I'm afraid the telephone is somewhat unreliable on the island, miss,' he said calmly. 'No doubt it will be restored to good working order eventually. I have taken steps to inform the telephone company.'

Suki tried to read his face and failed. He might be telling the truth and, if he wasn't, she wasn't going to find any evidence of that in his dark eyes. She slowly sat down and looked along the table. Joel seated himself and flicked out his napkin, meeting her stare with a cool amusement which was infuriating.

'Too bad,' he murmured mockingly. 'Was your call urgent?'

'Yes,' she said. 'I wanted to ring for a car to take me to the hotel.'

FitzGerald placed a beautifully arranged fruit cocktail in front of her, the elegant slices of melon, orange, grapefruit and banana coiled in a spiral topped by a glacé cherry.

Suki was waiting for Joel to react to what she had said and she looked blankly at the fruit while Fitz-Gerald walked around the table and placed a similar bowl of fruit in front of Joel. It was only when Fitz-Gerald had left the room, closing the door behind him, that Joel said softly: 'You aren't going anywhere, Suki.'

Her fingers clenched around the spoon as if she was going to throw it at him. She had expected just such an answer, but she was furious to have got it. 'Who says?' she retorted, lifting her head on a defiant movement, her green eyes flashing along the table towards him.

'I do.' Joel smiled drily and began to eat, while she watched his bent black head with a sensation of prickling alarm.

'You can't stop me. You don't honestly think I'm going to stay here with you, do you? I'm packing and then I'm going and I want a car to take me to the hotel.'

'You aren't getting a car,' Joel said casually. 'And

you aren't leaving. You're staying right here.' His lashes flicked upward, the steel of his glance shooting over her, then he looked down again and went on eating while Suki stared at him, her skin going ice-cold with nerves.

CHAPTER NINE

WHILE she was searching her disturbed mind for a retort convincing enough to make him realise he couldn't enforce that calm threat, Joel changed the subject, taking her by surprise again. 'How do you feel about the news that Rosie's going to have a baby? Going to put your nose out of joint, isn't it?'

'I'm very glad for them,' Suki flung back, and he looked at her with a mocking little smile.

'Are you?'

'Yes,' she insisted.

'I don't believe it,' said Joel. 'They aren't going to centre their whole lives on you any more and you're beginning to realise it, aren't you? You're beginning to see that things are going to be very different from now on—look at this holiday, for a start. They were coming too, weren't they? They've always gone everywhere with you until now. They haven't let you move an inch without them, for years. I picked that up the night I had dinner at their house.'

'I'm not discussing Buddy and Rosie with you!'

'You're discussing what I want to discuss,' Joel drawled coolly.

Suki glared at him, eyes catlike, wide and green and angry, but that look merely made him amused.

'I can understand how it started,' said Joel. 'You needed them at the beginning—you were far too young to be allowed to go anywhere without protection, especially in the music business.' His dark brows met and he stared at the table in silence for a moment. 'I've seen too many young kids destroyed before they had a chance to get anywhere. There are sharks behind every rock in that world.' He looked up, grimacing. 'You were lucky to meet Buddy the way you did.'

'I know I was,' Suki agreed. 'He and Rosie have been fantastic to me. I owe them my career.'

'And they owe you,' Joel said tersely. 'You were an uncut diamond and Buddy just picked you up in the street. He smoothed off your rough edges and gave you the setting to show you off—but he didn't make you, Suki. You did as much for him as he did for you.'

'Don't be ridiculous!'

'You gave him power,' said Joel, his mouth twisting. 'With you in his stable he was really at the top and coining money, people in the business had to start listening to him, taking him seriously. You know what a difference having you has made to his life style. You aren't stupid. You've doubled his income every year since he found you.'

'Oh, money,' Suki muttered, her expression impatient. 'What about my income? Over the last year I've . . .'

'I can imagine,' Joel cut in, halting her. 'Okay, you've done each other favours, you owe each other, it's mutual. But you aren't a puppet, you're an adult woman now, and it's time you cut the strings Buddy has pulled ever since you were seventeen. Start walking free, Suki.'

'I've always been free,' Suki protested. 'If Buddy ran

my life it was with my consent, he didn't force me to do anything, he never did. It was always a partnership, I knew he wanted what was best for me and I trusted him and Rosie. There has to be trust somewhere, otherwise you can never be sure that what you're doing is going to be right.'

'You let them take over too much, though,' Joel said roughly. 'You never developed as a person, you stayed a seventeen-year-old.'

'You don't know what you're talking about!' She sat upright, her green eyes bitterly angry.

'Don't I?' He moved and she knew he was getting up, coming towards her with some dark threat in his eyes. She shrank back in her chair, her breath held, then FitzGerald opened the door and Joel relaxed, wiping that tense look off his face as though by magic. FitzGerald removed their half-eaten fruit with a totally expressionless face and began to serve the second course. They ate in silence while he moved around, refilling their wine glasses, the silent tread of his feet a deterrent to any argument.

'What do you think of the villa?' Joel asked, and Suki told him she thought it was very beautiful, very peaceful.

'Wonderful to have a private beach all to yourself,' she said, and Joel told her she should be very careful when she was swimming because the tide was deceptive, you could easily be dragged out to deep waters by a current running very rapidly past the little bay.

'So FitzGerald warned me,' Suki said, giving the man a pleasant smile as he deftly whisked away her plate.

'What made you buy the place from Sir Humphrey?' she asked Joel deliberately, giving him a secret, mocking look from under her lashes.

She got back a thoughtful stare. 'I sold it to him in the first place,' he told her, surprising her. 'I regretted doing so later and I got him to throw the villa in with the shares I bought from him.'

Suki glanced at FitzGerald as he showed her a delicate confection of fruit and meringue. 'I see,' she said, then nodded. 'I'd like a very small slice of that, thank you, FitzGerald.'

He served her and moved away. So Joel Harlow had been 'the American gentleman' who had owned the villa in the past, she thought. FitzGerald was very discreet. She watched him serve Joel and then withdraw, closing the door.

'I'd already asked him to sell me back the villa before I met you,' Joel told her drily, and she was pricked by the amused mockery in his voice.

'If I'd known you owned it I wouldn't have come here,' she said, hoping to flick him and dispel that satisfied smile.

'I was aware of that,' Joel merely said.

'So I wasn't told!' she challenged, and he shrugged his wide shoulders with silent agreement.

She kept her gaze on him. 'You can't seriously expect me to stay here alone with you!'

Joel pushed his plate away, leaning back, a tall hard-faced man with eyes which bored through her and made her feel nervous and resentful at the same time. That was how she had felt the first time she saw him, she felt at once that he saw things other people did not see and that had thrown her into a state of panic which she had felt threatening her ever since.

'Let's get one thing straight,' he said brusquely. 'I'm not here to talk you into bed.'

She stiffened, forced to believe that rough voice, the piercing directness of his stare, yet remembering the way he had pursued her and doubting her own ears.

'No?' she asked with quivering contempt. 'You can't be surprised if I find that hard to believe.'

'If it was just sex I wanted I could get that easily enough elsewhere,' he said, his mouth harsh, his face filled with distasteful indifference. 'I've never had a problem finding women. If you have money you can get anything you want, it's only a question of price. Most people have a price, Suki, all you have to do is find out what it is and pay it.'

A painful flush filled her face, she looked away, sickness at the back of her throat. Joel watched her in silence for a moment, then said quietly: 'You don't like that?'

'No,' she said, not looking at him. She hated it, there had been a ring of icy bitterness in his voice, and she flinched away from the realisation of what sort of encounters had put it there. There had been many other women in his life, she had always known that, but it was one thing to know something with your mind, another to feel it with your blood, your feminine instincts. Her intuition was conjuring up visions for her which she did not want to regard too closely—pictures of Joel touching, caressing, possessing other women. The visions hurt her, filled her with raw painful emotion which could not be so simply classified by calling it jealousy. She did not know what it was exactly, her inner eye tormented by those images. A sense of loss, perhaps? A sense of something taken, gone for ever, the feeling so baffled and confused she did not quite know how to pin it down; she only knew she did not want to picture him with anyone else.

'What about your wife?' she asked huskily, and knew she was betraying something by asking, her eye avoiding his.

'I loved her,' he said quietly. 'But it was a long time ago, Suki, and sometimes I find it hard to remember her face. We were both very young and I'm not the man who loved her any more. I've changed, I've moved on, and all I have now is a faint memory of her.'

She listened, forehead creased in a frown. 'You've never married again, though.'

'I never found anyone I couldn't live without,' he said, shrugging. 'And I wasn't in any hurry to risk falling in love again—that's why I understand your reluctance to risk it. I've been there. I know it can hurt if love goes wrong.' He paused, then said in that low, husky voice: 'But if it goes right, Suki, it can make life magical.'

FitzGerald appeared to tell them that coffee had been served in the lounge and Joel stood up, walking round to Suki as she rose too, his fingers closing round her elbow. She felt her heart thudding in the back of her throat at the touch of his long fingers and was angry with herself. While they walked through to the lounge Suki mentally argued with that stupid, weak-kneed feeling which she could not shut off. When he let her go she hurriedly sat down on the couch, her eyes lowered, and Joel stood watching her, as though trying to read her expression.

Suki slid forward and lifted the coffee pot, filling both cups with strong black liquid. 'Cream? Sugar?' she asked, and Joel shook his head, extending one long, powerful hand. She put the cup into it and felt the tip of his fingers brush her skin. Hurriedly she withdrew and picked up her own cup. Joel walked round, his cup in his hand, and sat down, next to her, putting his cup on the table.

'Now that I've reassured you about my intentions, do you feel any easier?' he asked wryly, watching her.

'I'm still not sure what your intentions are,' she pointed out, turning towards him, shrugging. 'You've told me you have no intention of seducing me, that's all. What do you want from me, Mr Harlow? What are you doing here?'

'I've told you over and over again,' Joel said. 'I want to know you, I want to get inside your head, find out the truth about you. The night I saw you walk on stage in the black dress I saw a girl who made the air burn with excitement, but I've never seen her since—I want to know if she exists off stage or if what I saw that night was an illusion you conjured up out of thin air, a stage trick which you can only pull off when you're singing.' He was leaning towards her, his voice low and vibrating, his face intent on her, the grey eyes narrowed to gleaming steel she could almost feel in her flesh.

Her mouth had become dry, she was trembling, staring back at him, a tremor of nervous reaction running over her whole body.

'A night or two in bed with you wouldn't be enough,' Joel told her, 'I want what's inside your head, not a few hours' sexual satisfaction from you.'

'You're terrifying me!' she burst out in an uneven voice, and saw his eyes widen and flash.

'Why?' The word came back like a bullet and lodged itself in her, almost flinging her bodily backwards, the shock of the question so intense she couldn't answer, her lips parted, her eyes held by his and unable to look away.

She moistened her lips and whispered: 'You want too much.'

The brightness grew in those grey eyes. She couldn't understand why what she had said seemed to please him, but she felt the air between them thick with unspoken words.

'I want everything,' Joel said huskily. 'All of you. If that fire exists inside you and isn't just an illusion, I want to walk into it and burn up.'

The cup of coffee rattled in her saucer and Suki looked down blankly at it. Her hand was shaking. She swallowed, forcing herself to lift the cup and sip some of the coffee. There was a pause, then Joel turned and picked up his own coffee.

She had seen the threat of Joel's presence in purely physical terms until now, but although she believed him when he said he did not mean to talk her into bed, his real intentions were far more disturbing. She had guarded her heart for so long that it sent a shiver of fear down her back at the very idea of feeling it under threat. Joel was ruthless: he had told her so himself. He would never be satisfied with less than the whole of her, he would consume her, drain her of everything alive, and Suki was sick with fear in the face of his intention.

Finishing her coffee, she put down the cup and stood up. Joel slammed his own cup down as she moved away and shot after her, taking her arm between tight, punishing fingers.

'Where do you think you're going?'

'I'm packing and leaving,' Suki said.

He bent towards her, his face all angles, the taut concentration of his will in every line of his body. 'I meant what I said, Suki—you're staying until I've forced you to realise what's happened between us, what we could have if only you'll stop running away and being such a little coward.'

'You can't push me around!'

'If you'd listen, I wouldn't have to,' he said, his features full of a confused feeling which held a mixture of anger and pleading.

'I've listened to enough,' she said. 'Why don't you try listening to yourself and see what you think? How would you like to have someone talking to you like that? Do you expect me to be cheerful about being told you plan to be some sort of demon lover, swallowing me alive whether I like it or not? Do you blame me for preferring to hitchhike if I have to, just to get away from you?'

His mouth moved in a wry angry humour. 'Is that how it sounded?'

'Yes,' she said, meeting his eyes head-on in defiant challenge. 'I get the idea you wouldn't leave me a spare inch of myself. You talked about Buddy manipulating me, treating me like a puppet. What do you plan to do? Isn't that what you want? Aren't you accusing Buddy of the very thing you want yourself?'

He released her arm, but only to take her face between his hands, his warm palms against her cheekbones, their pressure hard and unrelenting, tilting her head backwards so that he could look down into her frightened, nervous green eyes.

'He was in my way,' he said tersely, and she drew a disturbed breath at the force of the tone. 'I could see they were blocking me, standing between you and anyone who tried to get near you.'

'I wanted it that way!'

'Yes,' he said in flat admission. 'I realised that in the end. Which raises the question I'd say is the sixty-four-dollar question—why, Suki? Why does it frighten you to have anyone come too close? Why hide behind a barricade everytime anyone comes within touching distance? Are you some sort of emotional cripple? Can't you relate to other people except on a very surface level?'

She tried to evade his eyes, her lashes sweeping down to cover her own, and Joel's fingers tightened, almost shaking her.

'Answer me!'

'Why should I? You've no right to insist I answer everything, you know as much about me as you're going to know.'

'That's where you're wrong,' he said. 'I haven't even started to get to know you yet.'

Her lashes lifted slowly and she looked at him almost pleadingly. 'Joel, can't you see—there's no future for us? It wouldn't work.'

His face glowed with a sort of triumph, his mouth not quite steady. 'You know you're admitting something, don't you?' he came back at once. 'You're accepting there's a present, even if you try to say there's no future. However you try to deny it, you know there's something powerful between us, there was right from the start. I wasn't the only one to feel it. You took one look at me and began to run—and there has to be a strong reason for panic like that, Suki. You were scared of what you felt, maybe, but you felt it.' He bent his head and as his mouth touched her own she felt a feverish drag of desire start up inside her, a hunger she had been aware of from the moment she first saw him and which she had been struggling against ever since, but which her mind had been helpless to silence. Her lips trembled as the bruising kiss deepened into a ruthless demand. She knew her lids were closing over her eyes, her body was shaking. She struggled to resist how she felt, but she was powerless, lost, torn from her moorings and launched against her will on a floodtide of burning feeling.

Their bodies swayed together. Her hands inched mindlessly around his throat and clasped in his thick black hair, holding him close, while they kissed with that devouring urgency.

He lifted his head, eyes half closed, face darkly flushed, his body shuddering against her. Suki had stopped thinking altogether; she clung to him, her parted lips burning where he had forced that wild response from her, passion making her green eyes smoulder and glow.

'That was only the beginning,' Joel murmured in a thick, smoky voice which breathed desire. 'You set me on fire, Suki, you make me want to let go and burst into flames even if nothing's left but ashes afterwards. Don't you know that's what you do to me, what we do to each other?'

Weakly she let her head droop forward, the pale curve of her neck bending until her forehead rested on his shoulder, and Joel's fingers lightly stroked the nape under her tumbled bright hair, his mouth moving just above the silky strands, stirring them with his breath.

'Darling,' he whispered, the word almost a groan.

'I can't,' Suki muttered into his shirt.

'Yes,' said Joel, and his tone had strengthened, firmed, because the way she had clung and responded had given him encouragement. He thought he was going to win, he thought he had finally breached her defences and got to her.

'Your family aren't going to accept me,' Suki said in a muffled voice. 'I couldn't be your wife, Joel, and I refuse to be your mistress, I don't want to have little bits of you when you've got the time for me.'

'Ah,' he said, lifting her head with a powerful hand, looking into her eyes with tender amusement. 'Now we're talking the same language. I don't want little bits of you either, Suki. I told you that, I told you I want a whole commitment, I want everything from you. As for my family—you won't be marrying them, you'll be marrying me—but why on earth shouldn't they accept you?'

'I'm nobody,' Suki said in a still, aching little voice. 'I'm a girl from nowhere, I don't know anything about myself—I told you that. For all I know my parents were criminals or monsters. Who knows what sort of people I spring from?'

'Have you ever tried to find out?'

'No,' she said meeting his steady, watchful eyes. 'And I don't want to know.'

'Why not?'

'I prefer not to!'

'Why?' Joel wasn't going to let her dismiss the subject like that, his eyes stayed on her face, searching, probing, and she hated it, she didn't want him to look at her as if he was trying to look inside her head. That was what she wanted to avoid—anyone finding out anything about her. Buried deep inside her head were dark echoes of pain she could not bear to have examined. She forgot them as much as she could. She didn't want them brought out into the light of day for Joel's inspecting.

'Whoever abandoned me was someone I don't want to know,' she said.

'You hate them, your parents, whoever they were,' Joel guessed quietly, and she took fire at the words, trembling angrily.

'What do you expect? How would anyone feel? What they did was contemptible, they deserve nothing but contempt, and that's all they get from me!' The bitter feeling inside her struggled inside the raw ache of her voice, and Joel put both arms round her and held her, tightly, without demand, reassurance in the way he surrounded her.

'But that isn't true, is it?' he asked gently.

'What do you mean?' She hadn't given herself to that warm embrace, she stood stiffly in his arms, locked inside herself, a prisoner of the pain she wanted to deny.

'If all they got from you was contempt and indifference, it wouldn't still haunt you like this. It's because you care so much that you can't give yourself to anybody else. You're afraid of being hurt again, of being abandoned.'

'Dumped,' she said hoarsely. 'Out in the street in the rain—why wrap it up in nicer words? Everyone walks off in the end, don't they? You can't trust anyone . . .' Her words choked and Joel's hands moved up and down her back, stroking and comforting.

'Even Buddy and Rosie?' he asked softly.

'Even them,' Suki said, and stopped.

'You do resent this baby, don't you?' Joel asked, and she said: 'No, of course not, I'm happy for them, but . . .'

'But it pushes you out into the cold again,' said Joel, and Suki gave a slow hard sigh.

'I'm not so selfish that I don't want them to be happy and the baby has made them happy, I *am* glad about that.'

'Be honest with yourself,' he told her. 'What do you really think you're looking for, Suki, if not love? The love you never had from your parents or anyone else in your life. It's what we're all looking for, don't you realise that? Human beings need love the way they need oxygen, it's the basic need of life. You've been starved of emotion since you were born and you haven't learnt how to give love, but I'm going to teach you, because all that feeling is there inside you and I need it every bit as much as you need the love I can give you.'

She looked up at him, tears burning behind her eyes, her lashes flickering fast to keep them back.

'Don't keep pushing me!' she wailed like a child. 'You're scaring the life out of me!'

'Good,' he said, smiling. 'That means I'm getting to you, I'm not just talking to myself—you're listening to me, Suki, and you're responding, however hard you may try not to.'

'What is it you're expecting from me?' she asked in a confused and troubled voice.

'Only what I'm going to give you—love; that fire you've kept damped down for so long, my darling, that's what I want from you. I know you're wary and touchy and hard to handle. I'm prepared for a long siege, but we'll get there in the end if only you'll stop looking backwards at a past you can't even see and start looking forwards into a future we can share together.'

She stared at him, biting her lip. 'Doesn't it bother you that you'll never know what sort of blood flows in my veins?'

'No,' he said. 'God knows what sort flows in mine—I have some idea for a few generations back, but before that there's just a blank. I may be descended from a long line of pirates, for all I know.'

'I wouldn't be surprised,' she said, torn between laughter and tears.

His eyes glinted with amusement. 'Frankly, neither would I. My father had distinctly piratical tendencies at times. Plenty of top executives have walked the plank with his cutlass prodding them in the back.' He curved one hand around her flushed cheek and smiled at her. 'But if it really worries you I'm sure we can find out something about your background. I doubt if any-one has really turned over every stone to find out who

your parents were. I'm pretty sure I could find out.
We could put a team of detectives on it.'

Suki felt something tighten in her chest. She hesitated and Joel waited, watching her closely.

'It's entirely up to you, darling. I don't give a damn
for myself. If it will make your mind easier why don't
you let me check it out?'

She closed her eyes, thinking, frowning. When she
opened them again she met his unreadable eyes with
a wry grimace.

'No, I don't want to know.'

'I think you're very wise,' Joel said gently. 'After all
this time it's unlikely that you would have anything to
say to either of your parents. It's a dangerous box to
open, Suki, and if you can only push that bad memory
to one side you can stop living like a refugee and face
up to yourself and the rest of the world.'

Suki stared at him and saw the formidable bone
structure, the clear hard grey eyes, the strong mouth
and insistent arrogance of a self-confidence which had
never lost a fight.

'You scare me, Mr Harlow,' she said at last. 'I knew
when I saw you that you were like a bulldozer, nothing
stopped you, you just flattened all opposition and rolled
on over it.'

His mouth twitched. 'I'm a man who knows what he
wants when he sees it,' he admitted coolly.

'Yes,' she agreed.

'And gets it,' Joel added, and she regarded him with
dry wariness.

'We'll see about that!'

He smiled at her, caressing her face with one hand,

his fingers light. 'Did you come here intending to break out, Suki?'

She frowned. 'How do you mean?'

'Young Richie,' Joel explained. 'You said you were learning to play, was he going to be your playmate?'

She laughed. 'No, Richie has a girl of his own at the hotel. He called on me to give me a message from Buddy.'

'Why did you give me the impression there was something between you, then? Trying to send me away, were you?'

'Something like that.'

'You must think I'm easily discouraged,' he mocked.

'You jumped to conclusions! I didn't see why I should deny them.'

He surveyed her with his head to one side. 'You aren't going to make it easy for me, are you?'

'No,' she said, smiling, and was sure she saw a look of satisfaction in his face. Joel had had things easy all his life, he had always only had to stretch out a lazy hand and what he wanted dropped into his palm. Suki wasn't planning to slip into his grasp like a ripe peach. She still wasn't ready to trust either to his emotions or her own. She had given up pretending she did not feel anything for him. He had wrung that admission out of her now, but there was a lot more to it than that. Joel wanted more than she was prepared to give him at the moment. He wanted to engulf her, consume her, possess her body and soul.

She looked into those hard grey eyes and mentally backed off from their demand.

'I won't give up until I've got you,' Joel promised softly.

'Thanks for the warning,' Suki said, and he laughed, sliding his arms right round her again and brushing his lips warmly along the heated skin of her shoulder, pushing aside the thin straps holding up the sun dress and exploring her body with intent enjoyment, his mouth slowly travelling downwards until Suki gasped and trembled and pushed his head away.

'Stop that!'

'You've got so much to learn,' he said huskily. 'And I'm going to be the one to teach you. I told you right at the start—I'm never going to say goodbye to you, Suki. The minute I saw you, I knew you were for me, you were the one I'd waited for, and nothing and nobody is ever going to part us. I wouldn't leave you if you begged me on your knees. I couldn't. I'm already past the point of being able to go, it would leave me half dead now to lose you. I'm sold on you, Suki.'

She looked into the darkened grey eyes, her pulses hammering at throat and wrist, trembling with a response she wanted to delay.

'Don't go too fast,' she muttered. 'Don't rush me, give me time, you're too much too soon.'

He kissed her fiercely, the pressure forcing back her head, making her throat ache. She caught his shoulders to steady herself, but her lips gave themselves up weakly to him. Each time he touched her, kissed her, the response inside her grew, feeding on the hunger and demand inside him, the two-way passion flowing faster and faster between them every time.

'It will happen,' said Joel in that husky, unsteady voice as he lifted his head and looked with satisfaction at her, and Suki looked back at him and couldn't deny it aloud any longer, her mouth parting to say no but staying obstinately silent.

Joel smiled, a quick, passionate smile, his glance flashing over her in possessive assurance. 'Yes,' he said.

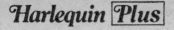

A WORD ABOUT THE AUTHOR

Charlotte Lamb was born and raised in London's East End. To this day she remains at heart an unswerving Londoner, although for the past several years she has lived on the rain-swept Isle of Man in the Irish Sea. Charlotte likens the Isle of Man to the setting of Emily Brontë's *Wuthering Heights* and says that all one can see for miles around are "sheep and heather-covered moors."

Charlotte began writing romances in 1970. Her very first attempt was accepted by Mills & Boon, and she has never looked back.

Since those earlier days, she has become amazingly prolific. Always a fast typist, she can now create and commit to paper at least one novel a month! "I love to write, and it comes easily to me," she explains. "My books practically write themselves."

The fact that Charlotte has been married now for more than two decades, and is the devoted mother of five children ranging in age from seven to twenty, immediately brings to mind the question: where does she find the time to accomplish all her excellent writing? "I have a very good housekeeper," she says with a smile...as if that explains everything!

 **The very finest in romantic fiction**

Get all the latest books before they're sold out!

As a Harlequin subscriber you actually receive your personal copies of the latest Presents novels immediately after they come off the press, so you're sure of getting all 6 each month.

Cancel your subscription whenever you wish!

You don't have to buy any minimum number of books. Whenever you decide to stop your subscription just let us know and we'll cancel all further shipments.

Your FREE gift includes

Sweet Revenge by **Anne Mather**
Devil in a Silver Room by **Violet Winspear**
Gates of Steel by **Anne Hampson**
No Quarter Asked by **Janet Dailey**

FREE Gift Certificate
and subscription reservation
Mail this coupon today!

In the U.S.A.
1440 South Priest Drive
Tempe, AZ 85281

In Canada
649 Ontario Street
Stratford, Ontario N5A 6W2

Harlequin Reader Service:

Please send me my 4 Harlequin Presents books free. Also, reserve a subscription to the 6 new Harlequin Presents novels published each month. Each month I will receive 6 new Presents novels at the low price of $1.75 each [*Total – $10.50 a month*]. There are no shipping and handling or any other hidden charges. I am free to cancel at any time, but even if I do, these first 4 books are still mine to keep absolutely FREE without any obligation.

NAME _____ (PLEASE PRINT)

ADDRESS _____

CITY _____ STATE / PROV. _____ ZIP / POSTAL CODE

Offer expires July 31, 1982   SB478
Offer not valid to present subscribers

Prices subject to change without notice.